Annie tel⸻⸻⸻me
to the far⸻⸻⸻the
afternoon⸻⸻⸻ed
his teacup

'I want you to look at this, Henry.' She passed
him the bank statement.

He laid it on the kitchen table to read while he
drank his tea. All at once he frowned, set aside his
cup, and picked up the sheet. 'Hey-up,' he said,
'have you checked this?'

She was silent.

'Annie,' Henry said, 'do you know Emmerdale
Farm Limited is heading for the bankruptcy
court?'

LEE MACKENZIE

Another Door Opens

Emmerdale Farm Book 21

Based on the successful
Yorkshire Television series
originated by Kevin Laffan

FONTANA PAPERBACKS

First published by Fontana Paperbacks 1986

Copyright © Lee Mackenzie 1986
Front cover photograph © Yorkshire Television Ltd
Emmerdale and Emmerdale Farm
are Trade Marks of Yorkshire Television Ltd

Made and printed in Great Britain by
William Collins Sons & Co. Ltd, Glasgow

Chapter One

The elder Mrs Sugden was due back from her holiday cruise to the Canaries on the following day, so a little tidying up to the kitchen at Emmerdale Farm might have seemed needful. Jack Sugden, newly come in for his elevenses, was for the moment oblivious of the mess; he was reading the small ads in the local paper.

His son Jackie was riddling the Aga. 'This thing's nearly out,' he complained. No response. 'Hi! I say, the cooker's nearly dead – and so'm I, I'm dying for a cup of something.'

Jack roused himself. He glanced about. 'Staff on strike today?'

Jackie, a hungry lad who had already done four hours hard labour, grunted in annoyance. 'There's lukewarm water in t'kettle. Fancy a cup of tepid coffee?'

His father had come to attention. 'Open the front right up, Jackie,' he said. He was accustomed to the little habits of the anthracite stove. His son, who for most of his life had lived in a council house or more recently in a caravan, still had to learn how to coax a flame.

He did as he was bid but surveyed the cooker with a pessimistic eye. 'It'll take hours. Looks as if the ashes haven't been shifted for days.'

Jack got down on his knees to squint at the ashpan. It was true – the inlet was jammed with cinders. He got the poker and began to smooth them aside so that air could get to the fuel. Ash filtered up into the air. Jackie coughed.

'Dunno what Mum thinks she's doing these days! She should have emptied that last night.'

'Too busy nipping out to look at her lamb, I expect.' Pat was for the first time experiencing the joys of raising an orphan lamb by bottle-feeding.

Jackie began searching on the dresser for a clean coffee

mug. 'She's wasting her time getting fond of it. It'll only have to go to market same as the rest, won't it?'

His father was too occupied in flapping at the fine mist of ash to reply.

Matt Skilbeck, coming in at the door from outside, surveyed him in astonishment. 'Hey-up! Who're you waving to?'

'You, as it happens. Got any hot water in your kitchen?'

'You what? I'll tell you what we *have* got – a damp spot on the floor where your Pat has had to wipe up one of the baby lamb's little mistakes.'

'She's never taken it in your kitchen?' Jackie cried.

Matt grinned. 'She thought young Sam would enjoy it.'

'And did he?'

'Can't tell. There were too much commotion going on about the blessing on the lino.'

Jack laughed, but there was a little uneasiness in it. 'I hope she's not going to get soft over that lamb,' he said.

'Nay, I don't think so. She hasn't given it a name, tha knows. It's when women start naming lambs and calves that you know you're in for trouble when it comes to marketing 'em.'

'What did you come in for?' Jack inquired.

'If you're hoping for elevenses, forget it,' put in his son.

'Nay, I were wondering when you were coming back up t'field. I need a hand with that decayed hawthorn you want pulling out.'

'Coming back? We haven't even had our coffee yet!'

'Nor even a clean cup to have it in,' Jackie added.

He was vexed. Although he had never said anything aloud, he'd noticed how the standard of housekeeping had gone down in the three weeks since Annie Sugden left.

Matt, too, had noticed the deterioration, but until now had been too kindhearted to say anything. But he'd had it on his mind, and now he decided to voice his anxiety. 'Ma's not going to take too kindly to coming back to her kitchen in this state,' he ventured.

'I'll fetch Pat and tell her,' said Jack, heading for the

6

door. 'Where is she – still with Dolly?'

'Nay!' exclaimed Matt, answering both points in one word. 'I wouldn't . . . Women can be touchy about things like that.'

Jack paused, taken aback. 'Can't think why. The place needs cleaning up; anybody can see that. What's wrong with saying so?'

'Hm . . . Look, why don't we get stuck in, eh?' Matt began collecting used cups and plates from the table, the remains of breakfast. Jackie, taking the advice, began to run hot water into the washing-up bowl, only to find it too was tepid. Jack pursed his lips as he watched the others.

It was a funny way to run a farm, he had to admit to himself – to have the three working men in the kitchen washing dishes while the farmer's wife was out enjoying the company of her pet lamb.

But it seemed that the only way they were going to get clean dishes to eat and drink out of was to wash up themselves. And the same might prove to be true of the kitchen range and the dusting – but that was absurd!

Nevertheless, while they waited for the kettle to boil for the mid-morning coffee, the three men began on the washing-up.

Pat Sugden walked in while they were still engaged on the task. She stopped dead, gaping. 'What on earth are you up to?'

'Getting a cup to have our coffee in,' Jack said, annoyed.

'Why's the stove belting away like a furnace?' She went to it quickly, closed down the flues. 'Honestly – leave this place for five minutes and you get up to summat daft!'

Jack and his son exchanged a glance. Matt busied himself with the washing-up.

Pat took clean mugs from the dresser – recently placed there straight from the drying cloth by Jackie. 'If you'll all clear out of my way, I'll get your elevenses for you,' she remarked in a tart tone.

'Gee, thanks,' Jackie said under his breath.

7

'Where've you been, as a matter of interest?' inquired Jack.

'Looking at that sick calf – where did you think I was?'

'Last I heard you were in Dolly's with the lamb.'

'Oh, that.' She blushed a little. 'Yes, well . . . that's no excuse for you lot hanging about indoors. Haven't you got work to go to?'

'But we needed our coffee—'

'Well, here it is,' she said, slurping water from the kettle on to the instant powder in the mugs. 'Drink it up and off you go.'

Her son accepted the mug. He could tell by the feel of the pottery that the contents were only lukewarm. 'Thanks a bundle. I always did prefer my coffee cold.'

'Then you've got it the way you like it, haven't you?' She was genuinely put out with them. 'Come on, swallow it down and clear off. I want to get this place ship-shape – your grandma is back tomorrow.'

'Mebbe you'd like us to drink it out in the yard?'

'Don't be funny, Jack, just drink it and go. I've a lot to do.'

'We had noticed,' he murmured.

She gave him a sharp glance. 'What's that mean?'

'You do know that lamb's going to market next week?' Matt intervened in haste to prevent a tiff.

She paused for a moment in spreading the drying cloth on the rail. But when she spoke it was with complete acceptance. 'Yes, I reckoned so . . . '

'Bullocks going as well. There's more interest in store cattle than milk cows at the moment.'

'Oh? Why's that, Jack?'

'Stupid EEC policy, that's why – money in milk's gone down by ten per cent.'

'Can I come to market with you?'

He stared. 'Can if you want. You've never been very interested before.'

'Well, I'm interested now.'

'Is there owt to eat with this?' Jackie put in, eyeing his

8

coffee with distaste.

'Biscuits in the tin.'

'But they're shop-bought—'

'Good heavens, surely you know it's cheaper to buy biscuits than make them!'

'But they don't taste so good,' mourned Jackie, nevertheless unearthing three from the biscuit tin and putting them into his mouth one by one but whole.

'Jackie! Don't wolf food down like that! Come on now, the lot of you – drink up and get off back to work. I've a lot to do.'

Indeed she had. It had suddenly struck her that Annie and her father would be home within twenty-four hours. All the many chores she'd put off because 'there was plenty of time before Annie gets back', suddenly seemed to pile into a mountain that she would have hard work clearing away.

First thing was the washing. She'd meant to strip Annie's bed and Sam's the minute they left, and get the sheets on the line. But somehow – since it wasn't urgent – she'd put it off from day to day.

Up in her mother-in-law's bedroom she was appalled to see a layer of dust on the dressing-table. Good lord, how could that have happened? She'd been up here with a duster only a few days ago. No, wait a minute . . . She'd come up but then the phone had rung and she'd gone down again . . . And forgotten all about the dusting in the pleasure of a call from Sandie, her daughter.

She hastily fetched a clean duster from the airing-cupboard. She cleared the dust off the surfaces, without pausing to think that when she stripped the beds she'd set a new cloud of dust whirling.

Signs of her lack of organization were at that moment surfacing at Home Farm, where she'd had a job in the office for a while. Barbara Peters was trying to find a list to use as a pattern for the quarterly supply requisition. She wasn't being helped by the hovering of her boss, Alan Turner, manager for NY Estates.

9

'She used to put them under "W", I'm sure she did,' he muttered, arranging to stand very close to Barbara at the filing cabinet.

' "W"? Are you sure?' Barbara said, reviewing the initial letters of 'quarterly supply requisition' and finding no 'W'.

'Yes, "W" for wholesale, you see.'

'Oh.'

'It isn't strictly logical, I s'pose, but I think she found there wasn't room under Letter "S" or "R".'

Privately Barbara thought that, in that case, it might have been a good idea to have a sort out. Her silence bothered Turner, who very much wanted her to be chatty with him.

'Well, never mind,' he soothed. 'I'll dictate how it goes, and then you can type it up afresh and use that for your pattern from now on.'

With a nod, she picked up her pad and pencil from the desk and sat down, poised for dictation. Turner, who couldn't summon up the slightest memory of what the list should look like, walked about with his hands behind his back, looking businesslike.

'Well, now . . . er . . . Before we do that, let's just discuss a more important piece of work. There's rather a lot of it, love—'

'Do you mind not calling me that?' she interrupted.

He stared at her. Her expression was cool and only faintly displeased.

'Nothing personal,' he hastened to say. 'It's just a way of speaking round here.'

'I don't see that that makes it any better.'

He wanted to say, Oh, don't be so touchy. But the last thing he wanted was a quarrel with her. He couldn't understand why she was so stand-offish. He'd done everything he possibly could to let her know he found her charming, attractive, sexy . . . 'If you don't like it, I won't say it,' he promised.

'Thank you.' Still no smile, no sign of relenting.

10

'Is something bothering you?' he asked.

Only the fact that my marriage is a wreck, she thought. Only the fact that my father thinks I ought to get together again with a man I haven't the least affection for. Only the fact that I find you smarmy and shallow, and that if there were any other suitable job within ten miles of here, I'd be off like a shot.

'Nothing of any importance,' she said.

'Well, that's good. My first aim is to keep my staff happy.'

She suppressed a sigh. 'Now what is this special job you want done?'

'Ah . . . Yes . . . ' He went to his own desk, returning with a couple of very thick folders. These he placed in her In tray. 'Now that contains the documentation for the animals we're going to take to Hotten next week. A big sale, you understand – bullocks, milk cows, heifers in calf. NY Estates prides itself on the amount of information it can supply with any animal it sells, so I want you to go through those folders and type up a document for each beast. You'll find it all there – milk yields, pedigrees, the vet's reports – and of course all our animals have been seen by a vet at some stage, if only to verify they're in top-notch condition.'

He paused, eyeing her. It was in fact a very big job, and any mistakes would reverberate back from the auction ring. What made it all the more difficult was that she was a townie, who had no experience of the background of live-stock rearing.

'I see,' she said.

'You'll find samples of how it's been done before at the back of each file – we always keep two years' sales papers. If anything puzzles you, just ask.'

'You or Joe?' said Barbara.

Nothing could have been more neatly calculated to puncture his complacency. 'It's better if you ask me. I don't want Joe bothered with paperwork. He's got his hands full getting the stock ready for the auction.'

'When do you want it by?'

'Tomorrow morning.'

11

She was taken back. The sale wasn't until the following week. She understood in a moment that he was punishing her for not being more friendly. 'Very well.' She glanced at her watch. 'I wish you'd mentioned it earlier, that's all.'

'Oh . . . Will it take you long?'

Only about eight hours, she thought. 'I shall have to work late.'

'Quite all right. That'll mean overtime rates, of course.'

'Of course.'

He frowned. He'd wanted her to be pleased with his generosity, not take it for granted that she'd get extra pay. But he soldiered on. 'And supposing you finish eightish, we might—'

The office door opened to admit Joe Sugden. He had a sheaf of handwritten notes in his hand and he looked expectantly at Turner.

'Yes?' Turner said, sharp and irritated at being interrupted at a crucial moment.

'It's eleven o'clock.'

'I'm well aware of that.'

'You said you wanted to look over the sales animals.'

It was only too true. He ought to be out in the byres now, not chatting to his secretary about going out to dinner after some overtime. 'Have you got them sorted out?' he challenged, hoping Joe would say no, thus allowing him an extra few minutes to complete his ploy.

'You said we'd do that together so we could be in agreement—'

'In which case,' Barbara put in, 'hadn't I better wait until they're chosen so I know which animals to document?'

It was an utter defeat. Although it had come about by accident, Alan Turner felt they were ganging up on him. The only dignified retreat was to pull rank.

'You do that, then, Joe,' he said with a lofty wave of dismissal. 'That's down to you, really, since you're the farm manager. Let Barbara know, will you? And that gives me extra time to get to Connelton. I'll run my eye over the stock later.'

He picked up his car keys from his desk and sailed out.

'Run his eye over them later and tell me I've got it all wrong,' Joe said under his breath. Aloud he asked, 'Who's he meeting?'

'Search me. I didn't know he had an appointment in Connelton.' She got up to glance at the diary. 'It isn't here.'

'He doesn't write down all his outings.'

'His jollies, you mean?'

Joe gave her a sharp glance. 'We-ell . . . '

'It was the same at my last job. The boss had to do a certain amount of socializing.'

'He's marvellous on the old boy network,' said Joe, feeling he had to be loyal. 'He can always find someone to sell something to, or get something from.'

'I believe you,' she said. Although the words held no criticism, her opinion of Turner was plain in them.

Joe's eye had travelled to the two thick folders on her desk. 'What're they doing there?' he asked in surprise.

'I've got to do the paperwork for the sale.'

'*You* have? That's his job!'

She smiled, 'I rather thought it was.'

Joe nodded in understanding. 'Taken his measure, have you?'

'I've met plenty like him before.'

He began to turn over the papers in the top folder, thinking to give her a hint or two on what to include. 'Hey!' he said.

'What?'

'Quarterly supply requisition for last year. What's that doing there?'

'Filed under Letter "W",' she said, taking it from him. 'Thank you. I was looking everywhere for that earlier.'

'I'm sorry, Barbara. My sister-in-law never claimed to be any sort of an office whizzkid – in fact, I think she only had shorthand and typing from her schooldays, that's all.'

'And no filing.'

'Well, filing comes natural, wouldn't you say?'

To anyone with an organized approach, she thought. But

13

clearly Pat Sugden wasn't a very organized person. She looked at the thick folders of information for the sales papers: if those were Turner's work, he wasn't particularly organized either.

'You wouldn't care to give me a hand, Joe?' she queried. 'It's all new to me. I don't know where to find the important facts.'

Joe was bending over her to point to the salient features when Seth trudged in. He took in the picture of the two young people in close proximity, put two and two together, and made twenty-two. 'Oh-er . . . sorry . . . didn't mean to disturb owt . . .'

'Come in, Seth. What's to do?'

'I was supposed to see Turner about me birds at half-eleven.'

'Sorry. He's gone out,' Barbara said.

'Yeh . . . Thought he wasn't around,' said Seth, thinking of the scene when he came in. 'Well, what am I to do about that new grain for the chicks?'

'You'll have to come back,' said Joe. 'I dunno anything about it.'

'Oh . . . ah . . . right you are, then.' Out went Seth, telling himself it were only natural that young Joe should take a fancy to the vicar's pretty daughter, though it complicated things that she was a married woman. Not that that had ever stopped Joe, of course, because that Kathy Gimbel had been wed.

'This is a big job you've been landed with,' Joe said to Barbara, turning over the top two or three papers. 'I'd help you all right, only you heard – I've got to sort out the beasts for the auction.'

'Yes, of course – this isn't your job anyhow.'

'Isn't yours, either!'

'Well, I'll have to roll my sleeves up for it, that's all.'

'I feel rotten about this. But that stock is going to take a while, and then I want to go to Emmerdale and leave a box of chocolates for Ma – homecoming present, you know.'

'Oh yes, she's due back tomorrow, isn't she?'

'That's right.' And what she'll think of the state of the house, I dread to think, he added to himself.

'You get on well with your mother?' Barbara asked unexpectedly.

'You what? Of course.'

'She lets you lead your own life?'

'You can say that again. She has a thing about interfering – never pokes her nose in. Mind you, she's got a way of letting you know her opinion.'

Barbara sighed. 'I wish my father was like that.'

'Oh . . . Vicar's all right,' said Joe. He was a little in awe of Mr Hinton, always had been.

'Do you know what he's done? He's invited my husband to come and stay so that we can sort out our marriage.'

'Oh lord.'

'You can say that again. My father thinks it's the Lord's will that all marriages should last for ever. And mine's gone down the drain.'

'I'm sorry.'

'Oh, don't bother to—'

'No, I mean it. I was married, you know. I know how it feels when it's gone dead.'

She looked at him. She could see it was true. 'Thank you.'

'Anything anybody can do?'

'No. But Daddy doesn't see that.'

'It's his job, you see. He's . . . he's duty bound to try.'

'Oh, you don't know how lucky you are to have a mother who minds her own business!'

Joe gave her a sympathetic grin and left her to it. He had a longish job ahead of him, sorting through the animals to choose the best items for the sale – not the very best because they wanted to retain those for NY Estates, not the very worst because it must never be said that NY Estates marketed inferior stock. And somewhere in the day he must find a moment to get to Emmerdale with his welcome-home present.

At the farm, Pat had finished dusting upstairs. She came

down with a load of sheets and pillowcases for the washing machine. She dumped them on the sofa, then for the first time took a good look at the kitchen. It was a sight – there was dust on the mantelpiece and piles of letters, the sofa cushions had a stain where Jackie had spilled Coke, the floor needed scrubbing, the Aga should have had a good wipe over with cleaner, there were ashes waiting to be emptied, the wastepaper basket was full of old pamphlets and brochures, Jack's sweater with a hole in the elbow lay across a chairback, there were dead daffodils in the flower vase.

'I'll really have to get down to this,' she said aloud.

The words were almost drowned out by the sound of a car engine coming up the lane. She went to the door to look out for the visitor.

'Oh no!' she gasped.

A taxi was nosing into the yard, with Annie Sugden and her father in the back seat. Annie got out as soon as it stopped. 'Hello, love,' she called, helping Sam out.

'Hello,' said Pat weakly. 'Did you have a good time?'

'Oh yes, lovely.'

'Hello, Mr Pearson.'

'How do, Pat. Here!' This was to the taxi driver. 'Careful how you handle that – that's my bag with my souvenirs.'

The driver handed the bag to him. Annie walked into the house, saying over her shoulder as she went, 'Been managing all right, love?'

'Oh aye . . . fine . . . '

Annie stopped dead in front of her, so suddenly that Pat almost trod on her heels. Sam, coming in with his luggage, elbowed them aside. 'Eh, it's nice to see our place again . . . '

His voice died away. Father and daughter took in the state of the farm kitchen.

'Well,' said Pat. 'Welcome home . . . '

16

Chapter Two

The reason for Annie's early arrival was simple. She and her father had been offered a lift from Southampton Docks to Leeds by a fellow passenger, instead of having to follow the arrangement of the holiday firm and stay overnight in a hotel.

But Sam was rather of the opinion they should have stayed in Southampton as arranged. 'At least we'd have got a hot meal!'

'Now then, Dad,' said Annie, 'there's nowt wrong with cold meat and salad for a midday meal.'

'I were planning a right feast for you,' Pat said in apology, 'only your arrival took me by surprise.'

'Aye,' grunted Sam. He was still thinking in dissatisfaction of the hastily arranged salad, served with bought mayonnaise, and the cold roast beef which, though good, had been too meagre in its helping.

He went out to his shed to console himself among his familiar belongings. Annie said in sympathy to her daughter-in-law: 'It weren't your fault we got a lift—'

'But I wanted everything to be nice when you got here!'

Annie laughed. She had been shocked by the sight of her kitchen when she first arrived but was now actually looking forward to rolling up her sleeves and doing some housework. Cruising was all right, but a life of leisure became very boring after a while.

Joe came walking in from the back footpath about ten minutes after the washing-up was done. 'Hello!' he said in amazement, hiding his gift behind his back. 'I thought you weren't due until the morning?'

'Got a lift,' his mother said. She returned his hug with interest. Eh! It was great to be back with her family again!

'We-ell . . . Dunno as I should give you this, sneaking up

17

on us when we aren't expecting you,' Joe said. He produced the box of chocolates.

Annie's eyes lit up. Truth to tell, it wasn't often that she got presents these days. When Joe was at home and Matt was unwed, both men had often brought little gifts back from market or a day in town. You couldn't expect them to, now that the one had a wife and the other was living on his own. And somehow Jack always seemed too preoccupied to think of such things.

'That's lovely, Joe! They're my favourites.'

'Think I don't know that? And I know they'll last you about three weeks at the rate of one every evening while you do your knitting.'

Pat was surprised. Since she came to live at Emmerdale, she'd never once seen Annie dipping into a box of chocolates. It struck her for the very first time what a great change had been caused at the farm by the arrival of herself and her children.

Joe asked after the farm, left his regards for Dolly and Baby Sam, but said he must push off. 'I've got Barbara in t'Land Rover at far side of pasture – mustn't keep her waiting, we're off to a ploughman's at the pub.'

'Oh, Joe! Bring her in! We can manage summat for the pair of you.'

'Nay, I know what you're like when you say you'll give us a snack – three course meal, more like.' He patted her on the shoulder. 'Nay, Ma, Barbara's got to be back in the office in about ten minutes flat if she's to do the pile of work Turner's loaded on her.'

'Oh, him,' snorted Pat. She had a poor opinion of Turner, had in fact given up her part-time job with NY Estates because, as she said, 'The man's a little twister.'

When they got to the Woolpack, Seth Armstrong was there – still there, having arrived well over an hour ago. He was leaning on the bar, bending Amos' ear with his views on romance. 'Aye aye,' he remarked as Joe ushered in Barbara, 'here they come, the two lovebirds.'

18

'You what?'

'Haven't I just been telling you? I saw 'em, couple of hours ago – closer'n two leaves on a bush, in Turner's office.'

Amos looked at the newcomers. To his eye, they seemed friendly enough, but no more than that. 'Shouldn't you be getting back to work?' he demanded.

'I'm in me lunchbreak.'

'How long d'you get, then? Two hours?'

'One thing I've never been, Amos, is a clock-watcher.'

But as Joe approached the counter, he thought it politic to start a fresh topic. 'I hear you're sending off a big batch to the sale next week, Joe.'

'Aye. Amos, a pint and a glass of white wine, and two ploughmans, quick as you can make it.'

Amos frowned. 'I hope I'm never remiss in my catering for clients,' he replied.

'No, no, course not – but Barbara and me are pressed for time.'

'*Some* folk never seem to let that bother them,' Amos said, with a magisterial glare at Seth. Seth slithered off to the far end of the bar to harangue old Walter about the rise in bus fares.

Although in fact Barbara and Joe were as quick with their snack as they could be, they had come late to the Woolpack and were necessarily late on their way back. Turner had returned from Connelton or wherever he'd been, and was not pleased to see the office empty and papers spread all over Barbara's desk.

He went into the kitchen to see if she was making a quick cup of coffee, but she wasn't there. Vexed, he went to her desk and riffled through the papers to see how much she'd done. How dare she, leaving all this lying about where anybody could read the information. Confidential, it was, all of it. If she had to go to lunch she could at least put the things under cover. Thus, having found a reason to be really cross with her, he shuffled the papers back into their folders.

19

Barbara found them so when she returned about ten minutes later. The time was a quarter past three.

'So there you are!' exclaimed Turner.

'Oh – hello – I thought you had an appointment in Connelton?'

'I had, and I've seen to it. Where have you been?'

'To lunch,' she said, raising her eyebrows at his tone.

'Until this hour?'

'I went at two thirty-five.'

'Oh.' He was momentarily at a loss, and was about to berate her over leaving the papers out when she forestalled him.

'Oh, heavens, someone's put all that stuff back in the folders!'

'Yes, I did, and let me tell you—'

'But I'd got it all sorted out into categories! It took me an hour and a half!'

'You shouldn't leave confidential documents where people might see them.'

'People? What people! The only ones who come in here are you and Joe and occasional members of the workforce. They're not likely to sell our secrets to the Russians.'

She was annoyed but controlled it well. Alan Turner found himself feeling in the wrong – which was unusual for him and something he disliked intensely. But, unable to think of a response, and certainly not in the mood to apologize, he busied himself with some work on his own desk.

A dead silence ensued. Barbara stood at her desk, dealing out papers from the folders rather like playing-cards in patience. Ten minutes went past, a quarter of an hour. Nothing intervened to break the silence, not even a phone call.

'Want me to give you a hand?' he ventured at last, thinking it might bring peace between them.

'It's better if I do it on my own.'

Nevertheless he left his desk to come and hover at her shoulder.

His breath smelt strongly of brandy. She looked straight up at him. 'Had a good lunch?'

He drew back. 'I grabbed a sandwich. You?'

'I had a cheese and pickle at the Woolpack—'

'That's unusual, isn't it? I thought you said once you didn't care to go into pubs on your own.'

'That didn't arise today.'

The only person she could have been with was Joe Sugden. It was on the tip of his tongue to challenge: 'You went with Joe?' But he thought better of it.

'After a snack lunch, you'll need a good evening meal,' he began.

'I don't think there'll be much chance of that. I shan't get this ready by the morning if I don't stick at it.' She studied him, waiting for him to tell the truth, which was that the work wasn't urgent.

And knowing that she knew that, he couldn't bring himself to admit it.

'Well, then, I'll leave you to it,' he said. 'If there are any phone calls, take a message.'

'Where shall I say you are, if anyone wants to know?'

He frowned. 'You can just say I'm out on business.'

'Will Head Office be satisfied with that?'

It was like fencing. He knew she was more than a match for him, and it only made her the more desirable – the first woman he'd ever come across who could keep him totally at arm's length.

'Head Office don't need to check up on senior management,' he told her, with a slight emphasis on the last two words. 'And if anything comes up on the farm, it can wait.'

'Or Joe can handle it,' she amended.

Damn the woman! He went out, saying over his shoulder, 'I shall need a top copy and two carbons of that documentation by ten tomorrow morning.'

He didn't want to target his anger on Barbara, who might one day surrender to his charms. Instead he went to Ridge Farm to harry Joe.

Joe was at a table in the outer room of the Ridge Farm

mistle, checking through a list of cattle with the chief cowman.

'All right, Alec, what have we brought in from Raventop?'

'Them four, Joe, and there's Daphne Three and Mary Rose on the grass if you want 'em.'

'What grass? There's nowt to eat on the pastures yet, lad! Can't expect cows in calf to do well on that scarce little nibble.' He heard the sound of the estate's Land Rover. 'Hang on,' he said, and went outside.

Turner was winding down his window. 'Nearly finished?'

'You what? There's eleven steers to look at yet, and I haven't talked to Jesse about t'sheep.'

'You might have started a bit earlier! It's got to be done by late afternoon so Barbara knows which papers to complete.'

'It'd have been done if you'd been here,' said Joe.

Turner treated him to a cold stare. 'Just make sure you send the information to Barbara by five o'clock.'

'I'll see to it myself.'

'I said send it. You're needed to supervise the grooming of the beasts.'

'But they're not going to the sale till—'

'I want to see what they look like tomorrow. If we have to make changes, we need to know in good time.'

Joe glanced over his shoulder at the head cowman. 'You mind a bit of overtime?' he inquired.

'Nay, Joe, that's all right.'

Turner looked as if he would forbid it, thought better of it, and drove off rather too sharply.

'Somebody's stolen his nodden cake,' suggested Alec with a grin.

'Na'then,' Joe reproved, 'let's get back to the toil.'

It was a long day. The paperwork was duly sent off to Barbara – 'by carrier pigeon', Joe wrote on the envelope before he handed it to Bob, the junior hand – and the business of grooming the animals was taken in hand.

22

'Daft, is this,' Alec grumbled. 'It'll only have to be done all over again on Monday.'

'I know that, and you know that, but this cow doesn't,' Joe said.

'Some folk have got less sense than cows.'

'Some folk talk too much. Hey-up, Alec – don't put so much energy into it, we're not tarting 'em up for the Yorkshire Show.'

At seven-thirty it was done. Joe washed up at the tap in the Ridge Farm mistle, then drove down to the village. There he made a purchase or two, before driving back to Home Farm. The light was still on in the office. As he went in, he could hear the tapping of the typewriter.

'Who's there?' called Barbara sharply.

He made a quick entry, so as to set her fears at rest. She took her hand off the paperweight she had put close by as some feeling of security in the dark, quiet, night-time countryside.

'Is that any way to greet the catering service?'

'You had me scared for a minute.'

'Tchah! You always feel edgy on an empty stomach.' He held up his package.

She sniffed the air. 'Fish and chips!'

'Aye, and a couple of cans of lager. Don't say I don't splash out when I offer a girl a meal.'

'Oh, Joe! Oh, let me at it! I could eat a hedgehog with the spikes on.'

'Shall us be plebeian and eat off the paper, or shall I fetch plates and knives and forks?'

'Better have plates. If I get grease on these documents and have to retype them—!'

'Oh, aye – heaven forbid.' He went off to the kitchen to find implements. 'How you doing?' he called.

'I think I'm about on target. And after this, I'll get going with fresh vigour, as they say.'

'Aye, half-time and the bits of orange always helps.' He came back with the plates. 'Your father'll miss your cooking tonight, eh? I hear you're a dab hand.'

'Oh lord! My father!'

'What?'

'I forgot to tell him.'

'Gee . . . Ring him now.'

'Funny he's not rung me.' She dialled the number, shaking her head at herself. When the call was answered, she began at once, 'Daddy, I'm sorry, I've been kept at the office—'

'Oh, Barbara!'

'I'm sorry, it's a rush job.'

'We've been hanging on from minute to minute.'

'We?' And then she remembered. Her husband was due to arrive this evening. 'I'm sorry,' she said. 'I just . . . '

'How long will you be? I couldn't find any preparations for dinner.'

'No – no, I was going to make a soufflé . . . I'm sorry.'

Joe was unable to avoid hearing. He was surprised at the repeated apology. After all, it was no great thing, Mr Hinton getting himself something to eat. He was used to it, after all.

'When will you get home?' Hinton asked his daughter.

'I'm not sure. Nine-ish, I think.'

'My dear! What about a meal for yourself?'

'I'm having something now,' she confessed, watching Joe guide fish and chips on to the plates. 'You'll find the remains of that chicken pie in the fridge, Daddy; you could have that with tomatoes and . . . '

'Yes, yes, don't worry, I'll cope. I'll tell Brian you'll be home about nine, then.'

'Yes, all right.'

He waited for her to say, 'I send him my love,' but she added nothing more except, 'See you later.'

Joe didn't dream of asking questions. He put the plate of food in front of her and urged, 'Dig in.' He led the way with some abruptness, for he was starving.

She obeyed. The food was reviving. 'Oh, this is lovely,' she said.

'Best grub in the world, except for roast beef and Yorkshire.'

'Or bacon and egg.'

'Yeh, or a ham sandwich with mustard. I think your father used to eat a lot of ham sandwiches before you arrived on the scene.'

'Joe . . .'

'What?'

'My husband's there.'

'Oh.' So that was why the apologies.

'I forgot all about him.'

'That's awkward.'

'It must mean something!' she burst out. 'You don't just forget a man's coming if he's important!'

'Quite right.' He pulled the ring on the first can of lager and poured it into a glass. 'Here, drink up,' he said. 'Don't worry about the menfolk at home. You don't have to think about that until nine o'clock.'

'No, that's right.' What am I going to say to him? she asked herself. Her husband . . . He seemed almost a total stranger already.

'Cheer up. Life can't be all bad,' Joe said, 'so long as there's fish and chips.'

To her own surprise, she began to laugh. Genuine laughter, with nothing of bitterness or hysteria in it.

'You're such a comfort,' she said, and began to tuck into her food.

Chapter Three

The trouble with eating fish and chips in the office is that the memory lingers on. Next morning Joe came in from his rounds of the mistle and pig unit to find the estate manager hopping mad.

'Where's Barbara?' demanded Turner.

Joe stared. 'How on earth should I know?'

'It's nine-thirty and my secretary hasn't put in an appearance!'

'I think that might be because—'

'And what the dickens has been going on here? The place stinks of fish and chips!'

'Oh, well, as to that—'

'I've got the accountants coming here at ten o'clock. What are they going to think of this?' He seized the wastepaper basket, holding it out to show the greasy paper crumpled into it. He gestured with it towards Barbara's desk to indicate the coffee mugs on it, and in doing so toppled out the crumpled paper, to reveal two lager cans in the bottom of the basket.

'What's been going on here?' Turner shouted.

Joe had to look down to smother a grin. The tone of outrage would have suited the evidence of an orgy.

'Look, you asked Babs to do the documentation for the sale. It was all completely new to her and you wanted it by first thing this morning.'

'Yes, and where is it, I'd like to know? And where is *she*?' Turner was even more enraged at Joe's having used the name Babs, which seemed to indicate a degree of friendship he himself had never achieved.

'I should think she's having a lie-in to compensate for the way she slogged her guts out last night.'

'It's good of you to come to her defence, no doubt; but

how can you know that's the reason? Where's the documentation?' Turner flurried his hands around among the papers on his desk. He was demonstrating that the paperwork wasn't there.

'Look in the red folder. We were here until ten last night getting that done.'

Momentarily stopped, Turner opened the folder. Sure enough, there lay the neatly typed sheets of information.

'Now you know as well as I do that that's your job, not Barbara's.'

'If you don't mind, I know whose job it is.'

'You asked her to do it without giving her any kind of lead-in to it. She needed help. Even so, it took us until all hours—'

'And no doubt you'll claim overtime.'

'Too right I will!' Joe said. 'And I'll claim for the fish and chips I brought in for us.'

'Oh, so that's how—'

'Yes, that's how. Did you expect her to work flat out without a bite or a sup?'

'That was her affair – I don't arrange catering for my staff.'

'Nay, who's asking you? But you have to be a bit reasonable, Alan . . .'

Turner had understood that he had put himself in the wrong. He allowed Joe's appeal to calm him down.

'We-ell,' he said, shrugging about in his chair like a ruffled hen, 'it's a bit thick to come into my office and find it like a tip. And smelling like it, too.'

'Let's open the windows. Soon freshen it up.' Joe suited the action to the words.

'But where is she?'

Sitting at home having a long talk with her husband, happen, Joe thought. But he knew Barbara wouldn't want her private affairs discussed with Turner. He picked up the wastepaper basket, put all the rubbish back in it, and took it out to the kitchen, where he put the contents into the pedal bin. Turner followed with the coffee mugs.

27

'I need her here,' he muttered. 'I need some things to show to the accountants. Why doesn't she at least ring, if she isn't coming in?'

Barbara was in fact in her husband's car, not too far along the road to Beckindale. It was parked on the verge. Barbara was staring through the windscreen, listening to Brian's words, and thinking he must really be in earnest to have got up early enough to reach the vicarage before she left for work. He had come from the hotel in Connelton.

'I'm not complaining that you didn't get home last night until I'd packed it in and gone. Okay, your job is important to you—'

'Not all that much,' she put in. She had to be honest.

'Why on earth did you stop there slaving away at these confounded papers, then?'

'It was a challenge. I was showing somebody he couldn't get the better of me.'

'Who, your boss? He sounds a charmer.'

'He is, rather. But he's the only boss I've got and I have to keep him straight about things.'

'Oh come on, Babs! You don't have to stay here in this one-eyed spot and work for a little Hitler.'

'Yes I do.'

'No you don't. You could come home now, this minute—'

'And then what?'

'We could start again, of course. That's why I came, Babs.'

She made no response to that, and after a strained silence he went on: 'I didn't mean all those daft things I said. I was angry at the time. You just didn't seem to be bothering about our marriage—'

'And you were?'

'I needed *something*, Babs . . . somebody.'

'And you found her, didn't you?'

'That's all over. You know it is. It would never have happened if we'd both been working at our own relationship.'

28

Suddenly she clenched her fists in her lap. 'I was working at it!' she flared. 'I was an ordinary, happy married woman with a job that took up her daytime hours and a husband who came home to her in the evening. I used to talk to you about my job . . . Until I thought perhaps it bored you and I stopped. It was a long time before I realized you never talked to *me* about anything except new tyres for the car or the cricket scores.'

He reddened. He was a handsome man, brown-haired and fresh-complexioned, smoothly dressed in a pair of expensive cords and a suede jacket. He drew in a long breath before he spoke again.

'I admit I was in the wrong. I didn't really like you having a job, I see that now. I didn't want to take an interest.'

'You said our marriage was boring!'

'Yes . . . I'm sorry. It was all a mistake. I want us to start again.'

She made no reply.

'Babs . . . '

'It's too early in the morning,' she said, shrugging. 'I'm not good at facing emotional appeals at nine-thirty.'

'Don't shrug it off with a joke. I've come all this way—'

'Oh, sorry if it's been a drag.'

'I didn't mean that. I mean, I've come to you, you wouldn't come to me. We have to talk about it, Babs.'

That, of course, was true. Whatever they decided, there had first to be a discussion.

'Look, I'll keep on my room at the Feathers. I only meant to take one day off, but if I have to stay overnight again, it doesn't matter.'

'Brian, will you stop talking as if I'm a problem you're having to fit into the business schedule! The claims department won't grind to a halt just because you're not there.'

'I didn't mean it that way.' She had this trick of putting him in the wrong, when all he meant was . . . Well, perhaps he *had* meant he'd intended to fix his marriage in one day flat.

She had changed. When she first walked out on him she'd been hurt and stricken, but now she was cool and though she had little spurts of anger, it was almost as if she was angry at herself for her foolishness, rather than at him.

She was more difficult to deal with than he'd expected. He thought that if he came, looking and truly feeling contrite, she'd soon forgive him. He'd always thought of her as a very conventional girl in the ordinary things of life, like marriage and social status. Now she seemed more self-contained than he remembered, and much more critical.

Well, he'd have to ring Mr Squires and say he needed an extra day or two. It wasn't by any means convenient, because there was that big claim on the building in Cardiff that had subsidence problems . . . Squires could never make head nor tail of surveyors' reports. But after all, this was his marriage he was thinking about, the basis for the rest of his life.

He didn't much care for the idea of going on alone. He'd got used to having a woman who got the meals ready and saw that clothes went into the washing machine. Stop-gap girls weren't the same – they had big ideas of their own importance, whereas your wife . . .

But somehow Barbara didn't seem like his wife any more. He glanced at her obliquely and found it odd that she used to scurry round after him, picking up his clothes. She didn't look the kind of girl who'd do that now.

'Tell you what! Let's go out for the day – go somewhere nice, have a good lunch . . . '

He broke off. He'd heard her quick intake of breath. She said: 'Is that your prescription for a mended marriage? Stroll among the abbey ruins, have a posh lunch and into bed for the afternoon?'

'I didn't mean *that*, Babs!'

She was contrite. What was the use of punishing Brian for her own lack of feeling for him? As to his feeling for her . . . She wasn't sure whether he genuinely loved her, or simply didn't enjoy the supposed freedom that had come after she walked out.

Did she enjoy it herself? Well, no. There was nothing here in Beckindale that made life particularly enjoyable. She wasn't a countrywoman, didn't particularly enjoy country life, and had very little in common with her father now. Her job at NY Estates couldn't be said to stretch her abilities – it was nothing like the zestful challenge of the property company she had left.

No, there was nothing here to make up for what she'd abandoned. Except, perhaps, her friendship with Joe Sugden.

That thought made her accept Brian's invitation to have a meal with him. She must at least consider what he was saying and not let herself take comfort in a friendship with another man. Joe was a nice chap – sympathetic without making a fuss, bright, easy to talk to. But it was well known that you could make the same mistake again if you were in too much of a hurry after the first one.

Brian dropped her at the vicarage, saying that he'd go back to the Feathers, ring his boss, and book a table for lunch. Barbara couldn't help being aware that her father looked at her with some eagerness when she came indoors. He was hoping, she knew, for a reconciliation.

But he had too much respect for her reticence to ask. And to put him out of his misery she said: 'Brian's staying over another night. We're going to have lunch together.'

'That's good.'

'Is it?' she said without enthusiasm.

In her room she picked up her hairbrush and sat down at the dressing-table to brush her hair. It was a soothing ritual. But it didn't have its usual effect. After a time she jumped up, snatched a raincoat from the wardrobe, and went out for a walk in the spring rain.

It couldn't be said that she was deep in thought as she threaded her way through the tangles of Verney's Wood. Ideas drifted in and out of her mind. Did she want to go back to the life she'd left? Had it been so desirable? But if not, what was she going to do? She couldn't stay here for ever, playing handmaiden to that little toad Turner. It wasn't even as if she felt particularly welcome in her father's home. The vicar walked round her delicately, as if she were some partly expired firework that might still have life in it.

Had she changed so much that she actually alarmed her own father? She sighed. They had once been so close – father and daughter, hero and hero-worshipper. She had admired him so much – his learning, his integrity, his dedication.

And now? Now he seemed a lonely old man in a country parish where very few really appreciated him. Certainly he seemed out of touch with the modern world. When he ventured opinions on items in the news – test-tube babies, trial marriage, bribery charges – he sounded as if he were talking about life on Mars.

She went back in time to change before driving to Connelton. Why she should bother to dress up for Brian wasn't quite clear to her. She certainly didn't want to attract him. It was perhaps to show him that even if she were living without him, she still kept up her standards. So she put on a wine-coloured dress of fine corduroy that brought out the clarity of her skin.

'You do look nice,' he said when he greeted her in the lounge of the Feathers. 'New dress?'

She shrugged. It was in fact an old dress, one he'd seen many times if he'd ever looked at her.

She made conversation about a fault in her car. He seized on it eagerly. He was very keen on cars. 'It's the carburettor again, I suppose.'

'No, the clutch. I'll have to have it seen to.'

Thus chatting about nothing, they got through the pre-lunch sherry. She asked him about his job. He explained that he was dealing with a very big claim, that assessing the damage due to subsidence was a very tricky business, that his boss was inclined just to take the thing at face value but that he, Brian, could see a fiddle when it was being tried on.

In fifteen minutes he told her more about the insurance

32

business than he'd ever done in eight years of marriage. It was amazing. But the sad thing was, it didn't make him any more interesting.

'Tell me about your job,' he said, sensing that he'd gone on too long.

'Nothing much to say. It's quite challenging, actually – all new to me, you know. I had no idea it was so complex, running a big farming estate.'

'What, getting straw in your hair, are you?'

'Hardly. Turner's getting worried about the firm installing computers.'

'Computers!'

'Oh, yes, agri-business – it's big scale.' She smiled to herself. 'Turner could easily be replaced by a computer . . .'

'I could say the same about some of the folk at Fortress Insurance.'

'About Liz, for instance?'

He went red. 'Now, look here, Babs. I told you that was over.'

'Oh yes?'

'I mean it.'

'You've never seen her since I left?'

'No-o. Never . . .'

She laughed. 'You're not even convincing!'

'Well, I mean to say . . . I've been lonely, Babs, I admit. Well . . . Once or twice. But I've never taken her home with me.'

'That's very sensitive of you.'

'Hang it, Babs, she doesn't mean anything to me! It's just . . .'

'What?'

'Well, she showed an interest! And let me tell you, she's considered quite a catch in the department.'

'Well, good for you. One more notch on your gun, eh?'

He sighed, pushed away his sherry glass. 'I want you back, dear.'

She looked down at the folds of her corduroy skirt. She

ran her finger up and down one of the lines.

'Look, it's so darned *awkward* here,' he burst out, glancing about at the other occupants of the bar. 'Can't we go up to my room and—'

'No, Brian.'

'But I—'

'Let's have lunch.' She got up and made for the arch leading into the hotel's entrance hall. He had perforce to follow her.

Being ushered to their table, furnished with menus, and choosing the food took up some time. It was difficult to pick up again where he'd left off. He consumed his soup in silence, considering how to pitch his claim. He hadn't done too well over Liz – somehow he'd admitted he was still seeing her, whereas his intention had been to say there had been a clean break.

Just as he was about to resume his pleas, the waiter came to take away their plates and serve the sole. He was growing irritated. It had never been his idea that they'd actually sit here and eat their way through a meal. He'd meant to persuade her to go upstairs, where a little physical passion might have pleaded his case better.

At last, when they'd eaten about half of the confounded fish, he broke out: 'This is absurd! Sitting here solemnly munching when what I really want is to hear you say you'll come home.'

She looked up. 'I don't mean to be hard, Brian, but . . . give me one good reason why I should.'

'What? What do you . . . ? Well, I mean, we're man and wife. We had a good marriage. We shouldn't let it go just because we don't make an effort.'

'We had a rotten marriage.'

'What?'

'You know it was a rotten marriage. We got married because it seemed a glossy, interesting thing to do – white wedding, champagne reception, pretty flat in an exclusive cul-de-sac, good wine in the wine-racks, cordon bleu meals to entertain business friends, posh weekends at the country club—'

34

'What's wrong with all of that?'

'What's behind it? When did we ever talk about the important things?'

'Such as what, for instance?'

'Understanding each other. Having a family.'

'Oh, if it's *that*—'

'There you are. You jump to an easy conclusion. I don't want a family, Brian. At least, I don't know if I do. I certainly didn't leave you because we had no children. In fact, I was thankful we didn't, because it made it easier to walk away.' She paused. 'All those things I listed – they don't attract me any more. I don't know if they ever did. So what's left? What should I come back to?'

'To me,' he urged. 'I've missed you. It's been terrible at home without you. Most evenings I've been round at the local, just for the company. I couldn't stay indoors by myself.'

'How many evenings, Brian?'

'What? How d'you mean?'

'It took you a long time to decide you were missing me.'

'Oh, for God's sake! I was angry at first – we both were! And I thought you'd come back when you came to your senses.'

'Come to my senses? Did you think I was so unreasonable to be hurt when you said our marriage was a bore and you couldn't be blamed for finding amusement elsewhere?'

'No, of course not. I've admitted – I was in the wrong. But I thought you'd gone off for a bit just to punish me. And when your father rang to say you were staying with him I took it for granted that by and by . . . '

'What?'

'I thought he'd talk you round.'

'Well, he hasn't. If there's any talking round to be done, it's down to you, Brian.'

'Isn't that what I'm trying to do? For the love of Mike, what do you want me to say? I want you back. We could start again.'

'On what basis?'

35

'On the basis that it can't be much fun here. I mean, I know you don't get on all that well with the Reverend.'

'Oh, I see. You feel our marriage is the lesser of two evils.'

He groaned. 'Where do you get all this from, all of a sudden? This talent for putting me in the wrong? What have I done that's so terrible? Other men have side interests and don't get this much stick for it!'

'It's nothing to do with Liz. I don't care about that.'

'Then what? What? I've said I want you back. What more can I say?'

'You could say something about love.'

'What?'

'Love. You must have heard of it. It's supposed to make the world go round.'

'Of course I love you, don't be silly.'

'I don't think so, Brian.'

'Look here, I know what I feel. I haven't dragged all the way up here just for the view, you know. I came because—'

'You came because you'd got fed up with an empty flat. It took a while, because at first you thought freedom was a great thing. But living on your own can be boring, so now you think you'd like me back. But I don't see any signs of grief for what we've lost or intentions to do better!'

'Me do better? But I haven't done anything so awful—'

'I meant both of us, Brian.' She sighed. 'That's the point. You don't see that it's both of us.'

'All right, all right, it's both of us. We'll try to do better. But we can't do that unless you come back.'

'I need some time on my own.'

'How are you supposed to have that when you're living in your father's pocket?'

'I thought you approved of that. He's your ally.'

'In his way, but all his talk about the sanctity of marriage is more likely to make you dig in your heels – I know you, Babs.'

'No, you don't. That's what I'm trying to tell you.'

'You're telling me that I'm too dense to understand you.'

'Don't take it like that. Nobody really understands anybody.'

'Oh, lord, don't get philosophical! I'm not here for a lecture!'

'I'm sorry you feel you're wasting your time.'

'I didn't mean it like that. But when you get your nose in the air like that—'

She laid down her knife and fork and got up. 'It's no use trying to talk to you.'

'Now sit down, Babs! Don't be a fool!'

'Goodbye, Brian.'

'Sit down! Don't waste all this confounded food.'

'What a shame. You'll have to pay for it, won't you? Never mind, you can save a bit if you cancel your room and go home straight away. And I should, if I were you.'

She walked out, hearing him behind her trying to disengage himself from the tablecloth and his napkin. By the time he reached the door of the dining room she was out on the entrance steps. She got quickly into her car and drove off without a backward glance.

She drove at random for almost a quarter of an hour before she paused to look at a signpost. She was heading in the wrong direction.

That seemed symbolic. Sighing inwardly she reversed and, taking side-roads so as to avoid an encounter with Brian on his way back to town, she set off for Beckindale.

She had almost got there when a thought occurred to her. She had been terribly anxious to avoid him on the road.

She'd said to him that there had been no mention of love in his conversation. Nor had there been in hers. The fact was, she didn't even like him much.

All at once she realized she couldn't face her father's anxious eyes. Instead of pausing in the village square to take Church Lane, she drove on and out the other side of the village, towards Loudwick. There it was market day. She spent some time looking at the activity, then found she was thirsty. She had a pot of tea in a little café.

By that time the market had more or less ceased action.

The little town began to empty as farmers and their families headed home. She shivered, felt lonely.

She ought to go home . . .

There was one little cinema in Loudwick, its canopy bright with a show of lights and a placard advertising a classic of her teenage years. She went in, bought a ticket, chose a seat at the side, and half-watched the film. She even dozed a little, for she'd slept very badly the previous night in expectation of having to face Brian today.

When she came out of the cinema, darkness had fallen. She felt fuzzy, as one does after a nap. She would have liked a snack, but the only places open in Loudwick at this hour were the pubs. She couldn't face the idea of anything stronger than coffee so she got into her car and drove off in the direction of Beckindale hoping to see a café en route.

But the only place she passed was a posh country house turned restaurant, where she'd be expected to order a full meal and which probably only took customers with advance bookings. She travelled on, troubled by a strange sensation in the management of her car, a lot of hesitation when she changed gear. She was about four miles outside Beckindale when the clutch packed up at last. She crawled to a halt, cursing her own lack of foresight – she should have taken the car into the local garage days ago. She glanced at her watch – eight fifteen. If she could find a phone box, the garage might conceivably still be open. But where was the nearest phone box?

She was debating whether to walk back, although she didn't remember seeing one, or trudge to Beckindale crossroads, where she knew for a fact that there was a box. But she reckoned it was about an hour's walk, and no fun at that in the dark.

A shimmer of light behind and the sound of an engine told her a car was coming. She stood in the headlights of her own vehicle, signalling for the driver to slow down.

Joe Sugden's voice said: 'Damsel in distress?'

'Oh, Joe! What a blessing!'

'That's me, God's gift to distressed damsels.' He was out

38

of his Land Rover now, making for the bonnet of her car to open it up. ' "What seems to be the trouble?" '

'It's the clutch, I'm certain. I ought to have had it seen to before this – it's been slipping.'

'Oh lord. Can't do owt about that in the dark. We'll get Bert Overton from NY's tractor department to have a look in the morning.'

She released the brake and guided the car while Joe pushed to get it safely out of the traffic-way. 'Hop in,' he invited. When she had done so he looked inquiring. 'Home, James?'

She hesitated. 'I . . . I was looking for a place to have a snack. But there isn't anywhere.'

'Woolpack?'

'Oh no.' She had nothing against the local inn but tonight she wasn't in the mood.

'Well, it's either that or fish and chips – no, hang on, Wilson's doesn't open today.'

'I'm not hungry. I just wanted a cup of coffee and a biscuit.'

'I know just the place,' he said, and released the brake.

When he ushered her into his cottage at Demdyke, he wondered if there had been the usual twitch of net curtains next door. But so what? It was only mid-evening. He cleared some farming magazines from a chair to make space for Barbara.

'Take a pew. How d'you like it – black or white, instant or real?'

'I'd love real, if it's no trouble. I take it black.'

He chatted with her in little shouts from the kitchen as he made it. 'Been out for the evening, had you?'

'No . . . I was out to lunch, actually.'

'Turner was hopping mad.'

'Oh heavens! I meant to ring him . . . '

'He rang the vicarage after a bit. I think Mr Hinton got a bit of the stiff side of his tongue.'

'Poor Daddy. None of this is his fault.'

'None of what?'

39

She didn't reply. He appeared a moment later with a tray bearing two steaming mugs, a bowl of sugar, and a tin. 'No biscuits, I'm afraid, but there's some of Ma's madeira cake in that.'

'Thank you, the coffee will do me.'

'Don't you think you ought to nibble summat? You look a bit peaky.'

'I'm all right.'

No you're not, he thought. She'd had a bad day. It was funny – under that cool, self-possessed exterior there seemed to be a very vulnerable spirit.

'Want to talk?'

'Oh no! Why should I load my troubles on you?'

'It wouldn't be a load. Besides, I've been along this road, remember. I know what you're feeling.'

If her father had said that, she'd have burst out in protest. But she had a notion that Joe was telling the truth.

'It's not knowing whether I'm in the right,' she said. 'Brian keeps on about wanting to "save" our marriage, but when I ask whether it's worth saving he never seems to have a decent answer.'

'I reckon your dad would say that any marriage is worth saving.'

'That's part of my problem. Daddy thinks it's *wrong* to say enough's enough. He thinks it's my duty to go back and labour at building it all up again. But how do you rebuild the ruins of Pompeii?'

'Oh, come on,' Joe chided gently. 'From what I gather, there wasn't any big explosion. The ruins can't be as bad as all that.'

' "Not with a bang but a whimper",' she said.

'You what?'

'It's from *The Waste Land*. "This is the way the world ends, Not with a bang but a whimper." '

'Cheerful stuff.'

She began to laugh. 'Oh, Joe, you're a tonic.'

'Ruby tonic wine, that's me.' He was pleased. She looked brighter, her colour was coming back. 'Speaking of that – how about a drop of something to go with the coffee? I've got some brandy.'

'Oh no. I've had almost nothing to eat all day.'

'We can soon remedy that. And I could do with a bite myself. Half a sec.' He went into the kitchen to examine what might be in the fridge. But the contents were poor, because his mother hadn't been at home to bring replenishments. 'I've got eggs,' he called, 'and cheese . . . And tomatoes, and a packet of bought ham . . . Plenty of bread . . . What about a double-decker sandwich?'

She appeared at his side. 'I'll make them,' she said. 'Out of my way.'

'Oh yeh . . . Dolly Skilbeck says you're a cordon bleu chef.'

She smiled. 'Not quite. But I do know how to handle food.'

She enjoyed fussing about in his kitchen. The double-deckers she made were enriched with fancy trimmings Joe would never have bothered with. They sat down at the kitchen table to eat them, helped along with a bottle of white wine.

The talk between them was easy and yet quite deep. She found she was able to confide to Joe all sorts of anxieties: was she being selfish? Opinionated? Did she expect too much of marriage? Should she settle for second-best? Or was her father's standard, on the other hand, too high?

'You have to remember that t'vicar's an old-fashioned Christian. He wouldn't marry my brother and Pat in church, 'cos Pat was a divorcée.'

'Did you think that was right?'

He hesitated. 'Well, as a matter of fact, yes. Because, you see, Jack isn't a Christian and Pat had actually promised to stay married to her first husband in church. If Pat was all that keen on having a ceremony in church, it ought to mean that she valued the first one – so she should have stuck by her vow. Can't have it both ways.'

'You think it's important, a church ceremony?'

'Who, me? Nay . . . I was only stating what I thought

were t'vicar's view. Nay, I don't think anybody should be tied for ever by a vow, wherever it's made. People change. Things you think you can live with for ever become intolerable. It's the same in business – you make a contract for a number of years but then you find it don't work so you have to renegotiate.'

'Renegotiate . . . Is that what I'm doing now, renegotiating my life?'

'Reckon so. And no wonder you're shaky about it. It's a big thing.'

At length she caught sight of the clock. 'Ten-thirty! I really ought to go home!'

'One for the road?'

She hesitated. 'Well, all right.' She sighed as she watched him pour the last of the wine into her glass. 'The longer I put it off, the harder it is to face the explanations.'

'Will he be waiting up for you?'

She sighed, nodding. 'I wish he wouldn't . . . '

Joe looked sympathetic. Although Annie prided herself on never interfering, it had been true that she was often still up when he got home in his bachelor days.

'The worst of it is, if he's up, I'll have to tell him all that happened today. And I seem to have been talking non-stop. I don't want to go over it all again.' She yawned. 'In fact, what I'd like is to curl up like a hedgehog and sleep until spring.'

'Perhaps you could nip past him?'

'He would hear. The house creaks a lot.'

Joe hesitated. 'You could always kip here. There's a spare bed upstairs.'

'What?' she said. She was too taken aback to understand him at first.

'Spare room – turn right at the landing. The bed's quite comfy, I hear.'

'You mean it?'

'Why not?'

'Oh, Joe, it would be such a relief not to have to—'

She broke off, flushing at the admission that she was so much at odds with her own father.

'Okay, I'll get sheets and blankets – plenty of those. Ma saw to that when I bought the place.'

He went out and up to the airing cupboard. He had acted out of an impulse of sympathy which he considered right.

He had forgotten that the curtain-twitchers next door would take note that his guest stayed overnight.

Chapter Four

Sam Pearson thought it good sense to leave the house as soon as breakfast was over. His daughter was planning a big clean-up, and he knew from experience that it meant vacuum cleaners droning, chairs stacked one on the other, the back door open while washing was taken out to the line, and so forth. No arguing with Annie while she was in her spring-cleaning mood.

'The house did get swept while you were gone,' Pat protested as she saw the preparations even while breakfast was going on.

'I know that, love. It's just, I want to settle things back the way I'm accustomed.' Annie didn't say that she'd been a little put out to find her pastry board in a different cupboard, with flour still hanging on it from the last use.

'Ma's longing to get at it,' Jack soothed. 'She's been away three weeks – she's got a lot of pent-up energy to use.'

Pat let it go. No use protesting she'd kept the place in apple-pie order – it obviously was untrue. Instead she turned her attention to her son, who had heard of a job going in Hotten Market.

'Has it got any prospects, this thing with Mayson's?'

'Aw, Mum! Part-time cowman? Have a heart! Any road, first thing is to get t'job.'

'That's right, Jackie,' his grandmother agreed. 'A lot of lads round here are looking out for summat, so you'd better put your best foot forward.'

So Jackie went out with his great-grandfather, he to catch the bus to Hotten, Sam to obtain some seed for an early crop of sugar peas from Ernie Plunkett, who had done well with them last year.

He said goodbye and good luck to Jackie at the bus stop. As he trudged along the High Street, he met Henry Wilks of the Woolpack out for his early morning walk.

'Off birdwatching, Henry?' he said with a nod towards the binoculars.

'Aye, glimpsed some stonechats on t'Struggle yesterday. I'm off up to see if they're nesting there.'

'Pretty things, stonechats.'

'Aye. You're out early, Sam. It's only just gone eight-thirty.'

'Spring-cleaning,' Sam said, as sufficient explanation.

'Oh, dear. I hope Amos doesn't get the urge. Last year he turned the place upside down trying to make it gleam with polished brass and copper. Hey, are you coming up to t'Struggle with me?'

'Nay, I'm going to Ernie Plunkett's. He lives along Butter Lane.'

'Oh aye, that's just beyond Demdyke Row. I'll walk that way to t'Struggle, then.'

They fell into step and were deep in talk about the prospects for Emerald's calves as they passed Joe's house. They probably wouldn't even have looked up at it but that the front door opened.

Barbara Peters emerged. She came down the short path to the gate. Both men slowed automatically.

'Good morning,' she said with a bright smile as she came out to the pavement.

'Good morning,' said Henry, surprised.

With a nod she walked off briskly towards the end of the road, heading for the vicarage so as to change into more everyday clothes for the office.

Henry was frowning as he turned to Sam, who had plunged back into the history of Emerald's calves. 'She allus produced small beasts, Henry, but they allus did well. I—' He broke off, looking at Henry in perplexity. 'What's up? Have I said summat wrong?'

'Nay . . .'

'Then why have you got a thundercloud—' He paused again. 'That were Joe's cottage the lass came out of!'

'Aye.'

45

'And that were Mrs Peters, Mr Hinton's daughter!'

'Happen she called in to give Joe a message from t'vicar.'

'At this hour of the morning?'

Henry gathered his wits. 'Summat to do with NY Estates – they both work for 'em, lad.'

'Oh aye! That's right!' Sam looked relieved. 'By heaven, I don't want to start seeing wrong where it don't exist. I'll be like Seth Armstrong if I do that.'

'No fear of that, Sam.'

'Aye,' Sam said, smiling. They parted at the end of the road, Sam once more back in the statistics of Emerald's offspring. Henry went up the steep stony slope to the Struggle, but his mind was no longer on the stonechats.

He was thinking about what Seth Armstrong had been hinting for days now, about a relationship growing between Joe and Barbara that he'd noticed each time he went into the estate office.

It so happened that when Barbara went into the vicarage, her father had gone to the church. An early morning phone call had alerted him to the fact that the recent rains had caused part of the churchyard soil to slip, making some of the headstones lean dangerously.

Barbara blessed her luck. She hadn't wanted to explain her absence. There was nothing to explain, really – it had all been quite innocent, her overnight stay at Demdyke. But there was her lack of consideration to apologize for. She hadn't even rung up to say she wouldn't be home.

The vicar surveyed the damage in the churchyard then went to see the verger. 'Billy, we'll have to get a team of lads to bed those headstones down again. Otherwise they'll be lying flat soon.'

'Scouts. We'll get scouts to do it.'

'While we're at it, could we plant a few flowers?'

'Flowers?' Billy said, shocked. 'There's daffodils – that's enough in a churchyard.'

'I think some summer flowers would cheer it up. Don't you think it's a bit sombre?'

The verger did not. He clearly didn't want to be involved with flowers. Hinton decided to discuss the idea with his chief warden, who happened to be Annie Sugden. Besides, he needed to discuss the arrangements for the christening of Dolly's baby.

At Emmerdale he found Sam carefully counting dried peas on the kitchen table, in the midst of the preparations for elevenses. 'Careful!' the old man protested. 'These are precious.'

'They look like the basis of good old mushy peas to me,' Jack said with a grin.

'Nowt o' the sort! These are sugar peas – best you can sow.'

'You mean they're sweet peas?'

'Nay, you know nowt!' scoffed his grandfather. 'Sugar peas – you cook and eat 'em, pods and all.' He nodded at Hinton. 'Your daughter'd know all about 'em, her being such a keen cook.'

'Probably,' Hinton agreed, accepting a cup of coffee from Annie. 'I'll ask her when I see her.'

'How d'you mean, when you see her?' Annie put in. 'She hasn't gone away, has she?'

It wouldn't have surprised Annie if she had. She had come unexpectedly and was just as likely to go the same way. Annie had nothing against her, but her impression was that Barbara was somewhat impulsive.

'Not gone away, exactly – but she went to Connelton to have lunch with Brian yesterday.'

'Oh aye?'

'To patch things up, you know. It seems to have done the trick,' Hinton said with quiet satisfaction, 'for she didn't come back last night.'

Sam gave a start which sent the dried peas scattering all across the table.

'What's up, Grandad – sweet peas gone sour?' Jack asked.

Sam turned his head away. After a moment he began to gather up the peas. When he'd returned them to their paper

47

bag he sat for a moment in silence. Then he got up.

'I think I'll just go and get these in,' he said.

'What, now?'

'Might as well.'

'But you haven't finished your coffee, Dad.'

'Don't feel like it.' He went out, snatching his cap from the hook by the door as he went.

'Something wrong?' asked Mr Hinton in bewilderment.

Annie sighed. 'I don't know. He gets these little moods sometimes.'

'Summat's upset him,' Jack suggested. 'Happen he's not got as many seeds from Ernie as he thought.'

'Nay, it were more than that,' his mother said. 'All of a sudden, something hit at him.'

The vicar still had to discuss next Sunday's christening arrangements with Dolly, so he finished his coffee and went next door, leaving the Sugdens to their little puzzle. He had no idea that Sam's distress could in any way be connected with himself.

The christening was a week away, but there were no problems. Dolly and Matt Skilbeck had invited Amos to be one of the godfathers, to his delight. He expressed it when Mr Hinton came into the Woolpack at lunchtime, bringing with him Brian Peters.

His son-in-law had arrived unexpectedly around noon. The vicar had been intending to sit down to a boiled egg and toast, but that hardly seemed suitable for a guest. The best he could suggest was to go to the Woolpack for a ploughman's lunch. Brian was quite agreeable. In fact, he seemed more subdued and less sure of himself than Hinton had ever seen him.

'Well, I was delighted with how everything turned out yesterday,' said the vicar when they were settled at a quiet table with their halves of ale.

'You were?' Brian said in surprise.

'Well, yes. It's old-fashioned of me, I suppose, but I do feel that man and wife under one roof—'

'Not for long,' growled his son-in-law. 'She walked out

48

on me within an hour – didn't she tell you?'

'What?'

'I thought you'd have guessed from her manner that we had a row. She was pretty upset, though you know she goes cold and quiet instead of bursting into tears like most women.'

'Brian, what are you talking about?'

'What I feel is, she's being more than difficult about this. I mean, I deserve some consideration for coming all this way. And though she told me I might as well pack up and go home, I stayed overnight again at the Feathers, and say what you like, it *is* an expense and a nuisance. I had to ring the office—'

'I . . . Of course . . . I understand you're putting yourself out a great deal, Brian.'

The younger man looked at him with a wry expression. 'It's funny, really, you being all in favour of patching it up. You never thought we should have got married in the first place.'

'I . . . thought neither of you seemed to understand what you were taking on.'

'Oh yes, the sanctity of marriage. That's important to you. Whereas I see now that if she and I had lived together a year or so before we took the plunge, we might have discovered we weren't really suitable.'

The vicar looked at the table. He was saved from a reply by the arrival of Henry Wilks with the food. 'You're staying at the Feathers, I understand?' he said to Brian, to make conversation.

'Yes, not a bad hotel for a one-eyed town like Connelton.'

'It has a good reputation,' Henry agreed, with a diminished desire to chat to him. Really, what could Mr Hinton's pretty, intelligent daughter have seen in a man like this? He was goodlooking, true – but as for manners, he could take lessons from a chimpanzee.

When he had left them, Brian sampled the crusty bread and cheese. After chewing a moment he said: 'I really came

49

to see Barbara, of course. I thought she'd come home for lunch.'

'No, she generally doesn't.'

'Though why I should make all the effort, I don't really see. I can tell you, after she went yesterday afternoon, I damn near packed up and left.'

'Ye-es.' Hinton sought about among the accoutrements brought by Henry. 'Excuse me, no salt.' He went to the bar. Henry was busying himself polishing glasses.

'Henry, has Barbara been in for lunch today?'

'Not so far.'

'You don't happen to have seen her?'

Henry hesitated. But facts were facts and bound to become known, whatever they might mean. 'I saw her outside Demdyke this morning.'

'This morning?'

'As I were going past soon after eight.'

Mr Hinton picked up the salt cellar. 'Thank you,' he said, and went back to Brian.

'What I'd better do,' Brian said as his father-in-law resumed his place, 'I'd better go up to this farm office and talk to her.'

'I shouldn't, Brian.'

'Why not?'

'Well – Mr Turner doesn't like casual visitors.'

'But this is the lunch hour. Presumably she does get time off to eat!'

'I suppose so, but . . . She might very well have driven to Hotten for lunch – there are a couple of quite good cafés there.'

'What a place,' grunted Brian. 'Lunching in a caff – it's not what Barbara's used to.'

For the first time it occurred to the vicar that his daughter was in fact accustomed to a quite different way of life. It was a measure, then, of her reluctance to take up her marriage again that she should put up with the deficiencies of Beckindale.

'Look, what am I supposed to do, then?' Brian

demanded in an exasperated tone. 'I invite her to lunch, she walks out, I come here after her and she's nowhere about. What do you suggest?'

Hinton sighed. All his instincts as a father urged him to tell this sulky young man to go away and leave his daughter alone. But his instincts as a priest were to preserve the marriage they had so rashly entered into.

'Leave it a bit, Brian. If, as you say, she was very upset yesterday, it may take a while . . . '

'You speak as if you didn't even notice she was in a state.'

'I wasn't aware of it,' he agreed, skirting round the need to admit he hadn't seen Barbara at all.

She at that moment was in the lane outside Beckindale with Joe and Bert, the mechanic from NY Estates' repair depot. 'I can soon see to that,' the mechanic said with satisfaction. 'I'll just tow her into the repair yard and do it up. You can collect it this evening, miss.'

'Thank you.' She and Joe stood to watch the car being slowly removed from its overnight position. 'It's handy having someone on the firm who can do jobs like that!'

'Oh aye, a big concern like NY can offer all kinds of little perks. Some problems too, of course.'

She knew he was referring to Turner, who had been absolutely glacial to Barbara when she first arrived. 'I should like an apology for leaving me absolutely without office staff yesterday,' were his opening words.

'Yes, I owe you that. I'm very sorry. I should have rung.'

'Yes, you should. And as you don't seem to be suggesting you were sick, I shall deduct a day's pay.'

'Very well.'

He'd expected her to protest at that. Her complete acceptance floored him. When Joe had happened by about ten o'clock to pass on some reports from his morning round, the atmosphere in the office was strained and silent.

'There's a tree gone over on its side and broken the wall at Hither Field – due to all the rain.'

'Very well, get a team of men with a tractor to drag it away.'

'Yes, I've put that in hand. The wall will take some time to repair—'

'You've heard of hurdles, I suppose?'

'Oh, yes, I've had the gap blocked off. What I was going to say, Alan – the wood from the tree, it's beech; that sculptor at Connelton was saying he'd like some beech to put through a new seasoning process—'

'Oh, don't bother me with trivia like that,' Turner said, waving him away.

Joe coloured and went out. Barbara said, 'Don't take out your annoyance on other people. I'm the one who didn't turn up yesterday.'

Turner was taken aback. In general, people had to put up with his bouts of irritation. 'What amazes me is that you don't even offer an explanation!'

'I've apologized, surely that's enough?'

'I should have thought that a friendly relationship between employer and employee needed a little more than that.'

'I had to take the day off for personal reasons.'

'That could mean anything from having your hair done to attending a funeral.'

'I should think you could see I didn't have my hair done,' she said, with faint, cold amusement. 'And I assure you it wasn't a funeral.' Although perhaps there was a death, she added inwardly – the death of my marriage.

'Very well, let's leave it. You don't wish to tell me and though I thought we were friends enough to—'

'Oh, if you must know,' she broke in, since nothing else would do, 'my husband arrived unexpectedly to try for a reconciliation.'

'Oh!'

She immediately went back to her typing. Turner sat for a time feeling a fool, and annoyed because he knew he'd been an interfering busybody. At length he said in a subdued tone: 'Er . . . Barbara?'

'Yes?'

'I'm sorry about yesterday. I'd no idea you were in that kind of a situation.'

She nodded, turned over a page of notes ready to start again.

'If there's anything I could do . . . '

'Nothing, thank you.'

'I don't know so much. At a time like this, a friend you could talk to is a great help.'

'Yes, I daresay.'

'I hope you'll look on me as that kind of friend.'

Not in a million years, she thought. 'Thank you,' she said aloud.

'My own marriage isn't so good,' he added, having at last found a way to get on less distant terms with this cool girl. 'My wife lives in Manchester, you know. She doesn't like the country. It causes a lot of problems, only seeing each other at long intervals.'

'I expect it does.'

'You and I have a lot in common, Barbara.'

She made no reply to that, but began to type vigorously and with concentration. Turner gave it up for the moment, but as lunchtime arrived he made another move.

'Perhaps you'd like to come and have a bite somewhere with me?' he suggested.

'No, thank you, I'm not hungry.'

'Oh, come, you must eat! And you're entitled to a break even if you don't want a meal.'

Joe saved her from inventing excuses by putting his head round the door. 'Bert's here ready to go and look at that car of yours.'

'Oh, thank you, Joe!' She jumped up in all too evident relief, seized her jacket and bag, and said over her shoulder as she went out, 'My car's broken down. Have to see to it.'

Now that the mechanic had it safely in his keeping, Joe drew her arm through his. 'What'd you like to do now?'

'How about a little walk? I could do with the exercise after spending all morning bashing the typewriter.'

'Word processor soon.'

'No, really?'

'That's the gossip. Headquarters is thinking about bringing in word processors and one of those linked-up computer systems where every farm office could call up information from HQ any time it wanted it.'

'I used a word processor for a bit in my last job. I quite liked it.'

'My word, you've seen the great big world, haven't you?'

'Oh, Joe!' She was smiling.

They walked on, down the lane then through a field gate on a footpath. 'You're used to cities,' he said. 'I've lived all my life in the country. Can't imagine living in a town.'

'Well, there are advantages. For instance, you can go and have lunch in a different place every day – and easily avoid people you don't want to see.'

'Meaning Alan Turner?'

'Meaning my husband,' she said.

'I thought you said he'd packed up and gone home?'

'I said I told him to. But I bet he didn't. He's a bit stubborn.'

Joe shook his head. 'I don't understand him. You've shown him you don't want to go back. Why not just make a clean break?'

'Is that what you did?'

'Well, yes. But we hadn't been married as long as you and Brian.'

She pulled a twig of young hazel towards her and examined the leaves. 'Everything's starting again because it's spring. I wish I could.'

'Why not? You're here in a new place.'

'Oh, I don't know, Joe. Beckindale just happened to be where my father had his parish.'

'You mean you couldn't settle here?'

'I suppose it's much the same as everywhere else. The people are the same, I mean.'

54

Joe laughed. 'Nay, country folk are different. You'll learn that soon enough. They gossip a lot more than townies, they take an interest in everything everybody else does. You'll see – I bet they've got you and me paired off and married already.'

'No!'

'Oh aye – they see us about together. Seth Armstrong were giving me a nudge this very morning – saw your car last night in the lane when he were out after a fox, took it for granted we were in the back seat together.'

Barbara began to laugh. 'That's nonsensical!'

'It's Seth. You better be ready for it when it comes back to you embroidered and gilded – he'll tell it to Amos, and Amos'll tell it to Ernie, and Ernie will tell it to his wife, and she'll tell it to—'

'Don't! It seems I'll be a scarlet woman.'

He joined in her laughter.

But it was more serious than they thought, for Sam Pearson had been deeply wounded by what he saw outside Demdyke.

All day it had nagged at him, since the vicar remarked that Barbara had not been home all night. By the time Annie was laying the table for the evening meal at Emmerdale, he had worried himself into a deep depression.

His daughter watched him aslant as he sat frowning at the local paper without reading it.

'Dad, we'll be sitting down to eat soon. Hadn't you better get it off your chest before the others come in?'

'What?'

'Don't pretend you're not worrying over something. You marched out this morning same as usual, but since you came back with those seeds from Ernie you've been like a wet week developing into a wet fortnight. Is summat wrong with the seeds?'

'Nay, lass.'

'Is it being back in t'cold after our sunshine cruise? You should wrap up well—'

'Annie!'

She gave up. She had annoyed him. He liked to think he was no softie, as well able as the next man to cope with the rigours of the climate in the Dales.

After a long pause he said, 'There *is* summat I ought to tell you.'

'I thought so.'

'Don't be so easy about it, lass. This is serious. It's about our Joe.'

She sighed inwardly. Her son was often at odds with her father, sometimes unintentionally, sometimes out of mischief.

'What's Joe been up to, then, Dad? I'm sure we can soon sort it out.'

'No we can't,' he said, shaking his head vehemently. 'It's trouble this time, worse nor it was wi' Kathy Gimbel.'

Annie experienced a faint alarm. 'What do you mean?'

'Our Joe is carrying on with a married woman!'

'Nay, now, if you mean Barbara Peters, that's just gossip. I think Seth Armstrong is up to his usual tricks—'

'It's nowt to do wi' Seth. I saw her myself, coming out of Demdyke this morning early.'

'Dad!'

'And you heard vicar say she hadn't been home all night.'

'She were at the Feathers in Connelton, with her husband,' Annie countered, although already she was beginning to doubt it.

'No she weren't. She spent the night in Joe's house in Demdyke Row.'

'Did you actually see her come out?'

'Aye, and Henry Wilks were with me. It's not something out of my second childhood, if that's what you're going to tell me! I didn't imagine it. She were there, and Henry saw her too.'

'Well, I expect there's an explanation—'

'An explanation? For her coming out at just gone half past eight in the morning? The explanation is that she spent the night there!'

He glared at her, daring her to prove him wrong.

And of course she couldn't. She could either believe Mr Hinton's version, or her father's – and her father had a witness to support his tale.

Chapter Five

Next day was Saturday, a busy day for everyone. Barbara Peters would normally have had the morning off, but had extra work to do for the sale of stock the following Monday at Hotten. She was getting her handbag and coat when her father came across her in the hall.

'Going out?'

'To the office – there's a bit of a rush on.'

'Half day or all day?'

'Can't tell, Daddy. See you when I see you.'

'You will be home this evening?'

'Of course!'

Her father shook his head in reproach. 'It's not such a matter of course. You didn't come home night before last.'

Barbara sighed. Here it came – the questions, the criticisms. Why couldn't he accept the fact that she was free, white and over twenty-one, and didn't hold his view of the conventions?

'Where did you spend the night?' he insisted. 'You weren't with Brian.'

'My car broke down as I was driving home in the evening. Joe Sugden came along, helped push the car out of the way, and offered me a cup of coffee—' She saw him flinch at this old cliché, and went on quickly: 'I spent the night in his spare room.'

There was a flash of relief at the explanation, but he asked at once: 'But that's only just along the road, Barbara! Why didn't you come home?'

'I . . . needed to talk to someone.'

He couldn't hide the hurt her words inflicted.

'I'm sorry,' she said, but angry with him for making her apologize. 'I had things to say that I . . . Well, by the time I looked at the clock, it was late.' That wasn't strictly true, and she went on, trying for total honesty: 'I just didn't have the strength to explain that Brian and I had quarrelled. I couldn't think how to explain it to you. I just wanted to crawl into bed and sleep – and that's what I did, in Joe's spare room.'

There was emphasis on the last words. She looked in challenge at Donald Hinton, who nodded.

'I don't doubt that. But I can't help thinking you were a little . . . insensitive to stay there.'

'To give the village something to talk about, you mean? Evil be to him who evil thinks.'

'I was referring to Joe's side of it. Is it fair to involve him in your problems?'

'He's not involved. That's why I can talk to him.'

'And I am, so you can't talk to me?'

'Daddy, you have your view of what's right and wrong. I understand that. What I can't and won't accept is that you want to enforce that view on me.'

'Barbara! I would never—'

'It's not intentional, I know that. But you can't just leave me alone to make my own decisions, because you're afraid I'll make the one that contradicts everything you live by.'

He didn't reply at once. She thought she was about to escape, and put her hand on the door knob. 'Wait, Barbara!'

'What now?'

'Oh, please don't take that tone,' he begged. 'You must know the thing I want most in the world is to help you! Please, if you need to talk, come to me. I'll be ready to listen—'

'As a priest?'

'No, as a father.'

She smiled with veiled disbelief and opened the door. 'I must go, Daddy. There's a lot to be done at the office.'

When the door had closed behind her Hinton was left with the feeling that yet again he'd failed to make contact with his own daughter. Why was he so bad at personal relationships? He longed to help with every fibre of his being, yet something always seemed to stand in his way.

Few were the people with whom he had a close understanding. His own son had gone away a long time ago to live a life that Donald Hinton could never approve of. Barbara, though what was generally thought of as a credit to him, had been growing away from him since her young teenage years.

He could think of nothing to do but turn to his God. He went to the church, pausing en route to watch the scouts energetically remedying the damage of the past heavy rains.

He had finished his plea for help and support when the church door swung open. Annie Sugden came down the aisle.

'Morning, vicar.'

'Oh . . . Morning, Annie. Something I can do?'

'It's about the christening. Could we do special flowers for the service? I thought all white would be nice. We've got some lovely narcissus at Emmerdale, and Mrs Brideley has some early white lilac . . . '

'That sounds fine,' said the vicar. 'I imagine you'll want to do the arrangements yourself?'

'Nay, Emma Courts is better than I am with difficult stuff like lilac – I'll ask her.'

He nodded, then put out a hand to touch her sleeve. 'I want to talk to you about something else, Annie.'

'Oh aye?'

'It's about Barbara.'

She stiffened.

'Now what's Dad been saying to you?' she began as he led her to a place in the front pew.

'Sam? Nothing, recently – why?'

'Oh, he said summat to me . . . Go on, vicar.'

Donald Hinton plunged in. 'I know I can speak frankly and you'll understand my intentions, Annie – not take offence, I mean.'

'Of course not.' She was puzzled.

'My daughter's having a hard time at the moment—'

'Yes, you mentioned—'

'Her husband Brian came here at my invitation to talk about a reconciliation. You'll appreciate, Annie, my great hope is that they'll get together to mend their marriage.'

'Certainly,' she said. It was what she herself would have hoped for, as a parent – *had* hoped for, when Joe's marriage began to go on the rocks. But hoping was one thing, reality another. She shivered a little in the cool church, bringing the fur collar of her coat a little closer to her face.

'Are you cold? I ought to get the heating going on Saturdays, I suppose—'

'Nay, go on wi' what you were saying, vicar.'

He sought for words. 'I find it hard to talk to Barbara. I – what's the saying? – I'm not on the same wavelength. And things aren't made better if a third party intervenes.'

There was a short pause.

'I'm sorry, I'm not doing this well. I find this hard to talk about.'

'The third party is our Joe?'

He nodded.

'I don't see what can be done, Donald. They work together. They're bound to see each other.'

'But you see . . . Barbara stayed overnight in Joe's cottage on Thursday.'

'Oh, I hoped that was—'

'In the spare room,' Hinton went on hurriedly. 'She told me that herself and I know it's the truth.'

Annie sighed inwardly. 'So Dad was right. He saw her come out, you know. He's been brooding about it ever since.'

'He saw her?'

'Yesterday morning, first thing. Henry was with him.'

'Oh dear.'

'And those neighbours of Joe's . . . '

'Yes.' Hinton couldn't give his opinion of the elderly sisters who lived next door and watched every movement – it would have strained his goodwill as a Christian.

'It could be awkward for someone in your position, vicar,

if this got to be common knowledge.'

To do him justice, Donald Hinton hadn't thought of that. 'Oh . . . Yes, I suppose it could be embarrassing. But I was thinking more of Barbara and Brian.'

'Yes.'

'Put yourself in Brian's position. How will he feel if he finds she's drawn to another man?'

'I think they're just friends, Donald. Really.'

'I agree – but Barbara's in such an emotional state these days that – well, she could easily lose her head.'

These painful disclosures had made Hinton restless. He got up and paced a few steps along the front of the pews. 'I ought to be able to help my own daughter! What good am I as a priest if I can't even help those closest to me?'

'They're the hardest to help, Donald. I know from my own experience.' She too rose, for she had other things to do in the village this Saturday morning. 'Is Barbara likely to stay in Beckindale much longer? I mean, that job with NY doesn't seem equal to her ability.'

'I think she'll stay for a while. You see . . . ' He shook his head. 'She really has nowhere else to go except back to Brian, and she seems determined not to do that.'

'All right, then, I'll have a word with Joe. It's not likely he can avoid seeing her altogether, him working on the estate . . . Still, I'll put it to him, Donald.'

'Thank you.'

The opportunity to speak to Joe didn't present itself over that weekend, since Joe was completely taken up with getting the stock ready for market on the Monday.

Barbara, who had spent a miserable Sunday mostly on her own, sought him out on Monday morning when he was hard at work putting the finishing touches to the store cattle.

Her excuse was that she couldn't read the writing on a report she was typing up. Joe borrowed her pencil to write the sentence out again in capitals.

'Turner says you ought to take lessons in calligraphy.

How's that for first thing in the morning?'

'Calligraphy – that's them signs they use in Ancient Egyptian writing, isn't it?'

She laughed, but sighed.

'He giving you a hard time, then?' Joe asked, quick to sense her depression.

'He's been ever-so-sympathetic ever since I told him Brian came here.'

'Well, that's better than niggling at you over every little thing.'

'He goes right over on the other tack, that's his problem. He was offering me a naughty weekend in a first class hotel in Wales, earlier on.'

'Was he, though? You should have accepted – it's easy to lose a type like Turner among the Welsh mountains.'

She looked momentarily vexed. 'Do you laugh everything off, Joe?'

He wanted to explain to her that her best defence against Turner was not to take him too seriously. That was the only way he himself survived. But of course it was different for her. She was just the right target for such as Alan Turner – a woman on her own, vulnerable, in an emotional dilemma, and in a position of inferiority.

He was saved by a call from Billy. 'You coming to hold this beast or do I do it myself?'

'Coming.' He glanced apologetically at Barbara. 'I'll collect the paperwork for this in an hour or so – I'll be off to the market before lunch.'

She nodded, shrugged, and walked away. He watched with sympathy – there was loneliness and depression in the very set of her shoulders.

When he came for the documents, she was pink with vexation. 'What's up?' he said, glancing about the office.

'I had to choke him off. Really, just because he's paying me to do the office chores doesn't mean he can take anything else for granted.'

'Don't let him bother you, Babs – it isn't worth it.'

'He's gone off in a huff, leaving me to check a pile of

63

invoices against the ledgers, but half of them aren't here. I don't see how it can be done before I go.'

'Go?'

'Oh yes, I've got this afternoon off in lieu of Saturday – and I'm going to take it despite his loading this on me.'

'Right! Get your coat, we're off!'

'Off where?' she asked in astonishment.

'To market. Better than hanging around Beckindale. 'Sides, I'll do the decent thing – I'll buy you a pie and a pint in the Red Lion.'

She cheered up enormously. 'Hang on while I just comb my hair.'

She spent a moment tidying herself up in the cloakroom. As she looked at her reflection in the mirror she noticed that she was smiling to herself – and all just because she was being taken to a local market to see some livestock sold!

Jack Sugden and his wife were off to Hotten also. Pat Sugden, newly brought to take an interest in farm animals by her dealings with the orphaned lamb, had asked if she could have a calf of her own to bring up.

'You sure you want to get into that?' Jack said, with a frown between his dark brows. 'You know on a farm we raise animals for what we get out of them. It doesn't do to make pets of 'em.'

'I understand that, Jack,' Pat said calmly.

It was true that since Sandie left and Jackie was out working part-time on the farm, she'd found a new interest in helping with the stock. Jackie teased her that it was frustrated maternal instinct; since she couldn't any longer cosset her children, she wanted to cosset lambs and calves. And there might be some truth in it, though she protested.

At Hotten they came across Joe and Barbara. Pat said significantly to her husband: 'There . . . what did I tell you?'

'Good heavens, Pat, just because he brings an NY

employee to see the sale of NY stock, it doesn't mean they're sleeping together.'

'Jack!'

'Well, what else did you mean by "There, what did I tell you?" '

'I only meant . . . there's something developing, that's all.'

I sincerely hope not, Jack said to himself. The last thing Joe needed was to get involved with a married woman – and one that his boss so obviously fancied himself.

'How do?' he said to Joe when they at last got close enough in the crowd to talk.

'Fair, fair. What're you here for?'

'Selling some lambs, and Pat wants to buy a calf.'

'Oh, "the wife's calf", eh? She going to get the proceeds for bringing it up?'

'Summat like that. You've got a lot of stock to sell today, I hear.'

'Aye,' his brother said, looking about anxiously.

'I'd like to have a look. Where is it?'

'That's what I'd like to know,' Joe said. 'Should have been here half an hour ago.'

'You what?'

'I left it all ready, waiting for transporter. Billy and his team only had to herd 'em aboard. I only hope the confounded thing hasn't broken down en route.'

'Hadn't you best do summat? Bidding's been going on fairly brisk already.'

'Dammit, I know that,' growled Joe. 'I'd best go and phone. Excuse me, Barbara.'

'Of course.'

'Happen you'd like to stroll over and take a look at what Emmerdale's putting in t'ring today,' offered Jack. 'Matt's sheep, mostly. He's got some good stuff – but then he always has.' He was only being polite; he'd forgotten that his wife didn't much care for Barbara.

Joe meanwhile got to a phone, no easy matter on market day. At first there was no reply, but when the receiver was picked up the other end, it was Alan Turner in a bad temper. 'Who? Oh, Joe – where are you, then?'

'At Hotten, where else?'

'Any idea where Barbara is?'

'Here with me.'

'With you? What the devil is she doing there? I need her.'

'It's my understanding she had the afternoon due in lieu of Saturday. Listen, Alan, never mind that – what's happened to the stock?'

'What d'you mean, what's happened to it?'

'Where is it?'

Joe could hear Turner draw in a breath and blow it out angrily. 'For goodness' sake, Joe, it's at the market—'

'No it isn't. I've been on the lookout for the transporter for nigh on three-quarters of an hour, and there's no sign of it.'

'What time did you order it for?'

'Me?' cried Joe.

There was a sudden silence on the other end of the line. 'I . . . er . . . that's your responsibility—'

'Hang on, Alan, you specifically told me to leave it to you because you had contacts with a haulage firm that could offer very advantageous terms.' It was true, and both men knew it. 'You didn't make the arrangement?'

'It's generally your job—'

'I know that, Alan, but you said this time you'd see to it. Let's forget all the ins and outs. Is there a transporter coming to Home Farm to fetch that stock?' He waited. No answer. 'I take it there isn't. Even if it came now it'd have missed the best part of the bidding.'

'There's no time to lament that now, Joe! We've got to get cracking to find a contractor.'

'You'll be lucky, this time of day.'

'I don't think it's much use trying to do it from this end. I think it's up to you, Joe.'

'Me?'

'You're there, there must be haulage contractors all around you—'

66

'Aye, and all with agreements to shift stock for some-body else.'

'There's no sense being defeatist. Get on to it at once – there must be *somebody* who'll come here and collect those beasts.'

'I'll see what I can do. But we'll have to pay over the odds, Alan, at this stage of the game.'

'Who's worrying about a little extra in the haulage charges?'

You were, yesterday and the day before, thought Joe. And speculating that your pal Holiworth would move the stock at five per cent less.

Angry and anxious, he plunged out of the phone box to hurry off in search of a driver and van free to take on this emergency.

Fifteen minutes of urgent inquiry brought him to Frank Dinsdale, who perked up when he heard Joe's question. 'It just so happens I brought in Lukers' lot and they're all going away with Holiworth vans. I'm free if we can agree a price.'

'Never mind that for the moment. Off you go to NY's Home Farm – you know the way? For heaven's sake get a move on – that stock should have been here an hour ago.'

'Right you are, guv'nor,' said Dinsdale, delighted at this turn-up for the book. NY Estates weren't short of a penny or two and this was an emergency – he could ask what he liked and be sure he'd get it.

An hour later, when most of the buyers had gone to the Red Lion and the Barley Mow for lunch, the stock arrived from NY Estates. Joe signalled it into an unloading bay. Jackie Merrick arrived to help unload the animals. Frank Dinsdale, who had done some quick calculations while he waited to see the stock loaded at Home Farm, presented his invoice.

'You what?' grunted Joe. 'This is a bit thick, isn't it?'

'What you worrying about?' Dinsdale said with a grin. 'Isn't your money, is it?'

'Estate manager isn't going to be pleased.'

'Too bad! He shouldn't leave things to the last minute if he wants low prices, should he?'

Joe was about to say that honest businessmen didn't raise prices skyhigh when other folk were in a bind, and also that NY Estates were unlikely to do business again with F. Dinsdale Haulage – but a uniformed RSPCA inspector walked up.

'Oh, it's you, Frank,' he said in an unsurprised tone.

'How do, Ted.'

'You dealing with this feller, Joe?'

'Aye.'

'Humph. Why d'you encourage him to do things like this? I'm surprised at you.'

'Things like what?' Joe inquired with a sinking heart.

'You know the regulations, Joe. So does Frank.'

'You're not saying I'm overloaded?' Dinsdale protested, too loud.

'Nay, I'm saying you should have had partitions up.'

'I were going to put up partitions—'

'Oh, that's the usual excuse.'

'Hold on, Ted, Mr Turner at NY Estates will confirm it! I were going to put 'em up but he said not to waste time, the cattle were expected at market, so I just—'

'Don't you worry, I'll speak to Mr Turner all right.' He turned a frowning glance on Joe. 'Were you there too?'

'I were here, waiting for stock to arrive.'

'Well, if we decide to prosecute Dinsdale—'

'You're not going to bring a case, Ted!'

'I've warned you often enough, lad. Pity you didn't pay heed.'

'I *did* pay heed! But Mr Turner said—'

'Did Turner say he wanted his livestock to suffer, being thrown about on those bends between here and the farm?' He was making notes in his book. 'Think on, Frank. You'll be hearing from us.'

Dinsdale turned his beefy, indignant face to Joe. 'Your boss'll have to pay that fine! I would've put up the partitions only he said—'

'Dry up, Frank,' Joe said in disgust, and walked away in haste to catch up with prices in the auction ring.

Pat Sugden saw him from the distance, and was glad he was too preoccupied to notice her. She was herding her own piece of livestock into the back of the Land Rover with the help of the previous owner. 'There, lass, she'll do you credit,' said he, closing up the tailboard.

Jack arrived back about ten minutes later. He looked fairly satisfied with the day's trading.

'Everything all right?' she asked a little anxiously. She would have liked a little more self-congratulation in his expression, in view of what she had to tell him.

'Not bad, about average – Matt's sheep never disappoint us.'

'Busy market?'

'Nay, summat went wrong wi' NY's input, dunno what Joe's thinking about leaving it so late . . . You want a cup of tea before we head back?'

'Nay, let's get off home, Jack.'

Something in her tone made him glance at her with perplexity. She seemed uneasy. He was about to start the car when a plaintive bleat rose on the air.

'What the—?'

He turned to look in the back. His gaze met that of a young Nubian nannygoat, whose mild eyes inquired when they were going to get home and offer her a more comfortable stall.

'What the devil's that?' he gasped.

'That's Annabelle,' said Pat.

'You've never bought a goat!'

'I have.'

'Pat!'

'Well, you didn't like the calf I sorted out because it wasn't fit enough, and all the others were too expensive so I . . .'

'We could have come another day and bought you a calf!'

'But she's lovely, Jack!'

'Lovely?'

69

'Ever so friendly. And Mr Byers says the milk is very sought-after.'

'Milk?' Jack eyed the kid. 'It'll be a year or two afore there's any milk from *her*!'

'Well, that's true, but—'

'What got into you?'

'She's a bargain, Jack. Mr Byers said—'

'There's no bargains without a reason! You shouldn't have bought her without asking me.'

Pat's chin became firm, her expression became mutinous. 'Everybody at Emmerdale has summat they do special – Annie runs the house, you and Matt run the farm, Dolly makes butter and does spinning and weaving—'

'So you thought you'd go in for goat-farming! It would have been a good idea to discuss it first, love.'

'Come on, let's get her home,' she urged. 'Poor little thing, she's fed up with being shoved around all day today. Let's get her home and in her own little stall.'

At the protective tone, Jack sighed inwardly. But this wasn't the time to argue it through. He set off for Emmerdale.

Joe was still at the auction ring. He and Barbara were listening with dismay to the prices being offered for the beasts from NY Estates.

'What's happened? They're far lower than anything I've typed up in invoices.'

'Bottom's dropped out of t'market. We're so late, you see – the dealers who came here intending to buy our stock got fed up – they're probably all on their way home by now.' He swore under his breath. What a day! First no transporter, then Frank Dinsdale gouging him for an emergency job, then the probable fine for insufficient care of animals in transport, and now prices that would make a cat laugh.

He signalled to the auctioneer. Watecombe raised his eyebrows. Joe shook his head and made a throatcutting gesture with his hand. Watecombe nodded and waved at

70

Jackie Merrick, who was about to herd in another fine steer.

'The stock from NY Estates is withdrawn, gentlemen.'

There was very little protest. None of the men round the ring expected to get NY stores at those prices – it was like crocks of gold at the end of the rainbow, it just didn't happen. There was some grumbling, and one enterprising butcher went off chuckling at having bought two grand beasts at give-away prices.

'You're withdrawing them?' Barbara said in astonishment.

'Nowt else to do. Can't sell NY cattle at that level – it'd be the talk of the region.'

'Joe, are you sure you're doing the right thing? I heard Turner on the phone to HQ, saying there wasn't another prime auction for weeks.'

'Not local, there isn't, but it's worth the cost to take 'em further and get higher prices, even if only for prestige reasons. We *can't* let our stock be given away – it makes folk think we're daft or summat.'

'Joe . . . ?'

'What?'

'How are you going to get the animals back?'

'Oh, lord!' groaned Joe. 'Well, I'm not using Dinsdale again, that's a cert. Hang on a minute while I look for a haulier.'

'I'll come with you.' In fact, there were several small haulage firms in the car park waiting about in hopes of getting a last minute job. Barbara kept each man in conversation while Joe went round the back to inspect the truck. With her help he was able to ensure he got a respectable firm and there wasn't any doubt that her smiling presence helped to keep the price reasonable.

When the cattle had been once more loaded aboard, Joe and Barbara got into the Land Rover to follow at least as far as Beckindale. Joe invited her to Demdyke Row for a cup of tea. She had been chatting about nothing all the way home. Now she said, 'You're really worried, aren't you? About what Turner will say.'

71

'One thing's for sure – it's all going to be my fault.'

'I don't see how you can say that. Even Alan Turner has got to admit you did your best in the face of his own inefficiency.'

'You don't know him! You've only been here a few weeks – you don't know how quick he is to turn anything . . . ' Joe shrugged and fell silent.

'Joe, whoever you work for, he's seldom perfect. Turner's just a few degrees more imperfect than most. But he *is* only another man employed by NY Estates.'

'Yeah – but he's my boss.'

'That depends whether you let him boss you.'

'What?'

'He gets the upper hand by assuming you'll let him. Even now, when you know he's to blame, you're worrying about what he'll say to make you feel bad.'

She handed him another cup of tea. Joe accepted it, put sugar in, and stirred it thoughtfully. 'Are you saying attack is the best method of defence?'

'Am I? I'm not sure. All I know is that if you treat him as if he's an equal, and sometimes less than an equal, he gets a bit less high-handed.'

'Huh!' Joe said, wondering if she could possibly be right.

Joe drove her to the engineering shed to collect her car. As she prepared to drive off she said, 'Off you go and face the lion in his den.'

'Yeah . . . ' He wasn't quite ready for that yet. 'I'll go up to Emmerdale, I think, see how Jack made out wi' the sheep.'

'Coward!' But she was laughing as she moved off.

At Emmerdale he found the place in a state of confusion over the nannygoat.

'A goat?' he cried when he was told.

'Oh, she's lovely, Joe!' Dolly exclaimed. 'Such a pretty little thing—'

'You must be mad!' Joe said to Jack. 'They're the most destructive things in creation.'

72

Jack looked fed up. 'What could I do? She'd shaken hands on it by the time I heard.'

'But what's the point? You're not going in for goats' milk, are you?'

'Not if I can help it.'

'You'll only have to get rid of it.'

'Don't say that to Pat,' Jack said with a grimace. He went out to join the admiration society in the barn, standing around watching Annabelle munching cabbage stalks.

Joe's mother was glad to have the kitchen empty, except for her younger son. For the last half hour it had been like a railway station with folk running in and out exclaiming about the nannygoat.

'Cup of tea, lad?'

'Nay, I just had some, thanks. I really came to hear what Jack got for the sheep.'

'He did well enough. It weren't a very good market, by all I hear.'

'You can say that again,' Joe said with feeling.

'Joe . . .'

'Yes?'

'I want to talk to you about summat.'

'Oh?' He could tell it was serious.

'Sit down, lad.'

He obeyed, feeling a little like his young days, when he'd been reported by his schoolteacher for teasing one of the little girls.

'Joe, what's going on between you and Mr Hinton's daughter?'

To say he was astounded would be an understatement. She *never* asked personal questions like this.

'What d'you mean, "going on"? Barbara and I are friends, that's all.'

'She spent the night at Demdyke on Thursday.'

'Oh, so that's it. Who's been gossiping to you about that?'

'It weren't gossip. Mr Hinton told me. He's worried sick about her, Joe.'

73

She should have taken note of the spark of anger that came into his dark eyes. 'Why has he got to make a big thing of it, then? She spent the night in my spare room, if you must know.'

She studied him, and made her second mistake. 'I believe you,' she said.

'Thanks very much!' He gave an angry laugh. 'Now that you know the worst, can I ask why you're cross-questioning me?'

'Now, lad, don't take that tone. Barbara's a married woman. You've got to remember that.'

'I know she's married. What's that got to do with it?'

'Can't you think of it from Mr Hinton's viewpoint? How's it going to look if people start scandalizing his own daughter?'

'Scandalizing? How can they start scandalizing! We haven't done anything!'

'Well, that's so, but the pair of you should have more thought for how it looks—'

'How it looks! Are you saying I can't be friends with Barbara Peters because a lot of rotten old gossips will take it the wrong way?'

'Now, Joe, you know it's not as simple as that. If you see too much of a pretty girl, you know you get tangled—'

'Oh, so I'm not to be trusted, is that it?'

'Nay, lad, I didn't mean it that way. But if nowt's going on between you, best keep it that way, eh?'

It was her third mistake, and the last he allowed her.

He jumped up. 'Great. That's all I needed to put a perfect end to a perfect day.'

He stalked out, leaving his mother staring at the closed door.

Chapter Six

From the conversation with his mother, Joe walked straight into a confrontation with Alan Turner.

The estate manager was at his desk when Joe got to the office about five o'clock. He had some papers in front of him, but pushed them aside. 'Well, I suppose I'd better hear your side of it first. Why did the stock come back to Home Farm in another hired truck?'

'Are you asking why it was a different firm, or why did I send it back?'

'The latter, of course. Please don't play games with me, Joe.'

Joe shrugged. 'By the time Dinsdale's truck got to Hotten, business was practically over.'

'Practically? I take it you mean the auctioneer was still functioning.'

'Aye, and taking bids that were a laughing matter. You wouldn't want me to give away NY animals? I withdrew all but the two that had been sold, and had 'em shipped back.'

'And you never thought to ring me for confirmation.'

'What could you have done about it if I'd rung?'

'That's not the point! When Billy rang through to say the beasts had come back and what should he do with them, I was taken completely by surprise. *He* naturally thought I was in the picture – and as estate manager, I should have been.'

'Is that all that bothers you?' Joe asked. 'That you were taken aback when the cowman rang through?'

'No, of course it's not, and I'm coming to the other things in a moment.' Turner threw himself back in his chair theatrically. 'And you had the nerve to apply for the job I'm holding! What qualifications do you imagine you've got for handling a section of NY Estates? You seem incapable of seeing the larger picture—'

Joe could hear Barbara's voice in his ear: It depends whether you let him boss you.

'Just because you made a thundering mess of the whole thing—'

'*I* did? Who took those beasts to market? Who withdrew them because the price was too low?'

'And who had a deal with Holiworth that was cheaper than the rest? And who never checked that Holiworth were actually coming to collect the stock?'

Turner's mouth almost fell open. 'Just a minute there!' he said, recovering. 'Your job as farm manager is to get the stock to market in good condition. Why didn't you check that the transporter was arranged?'

'Because you said to leave it all to you!'

'I may have mentioned Holiworth as a good possibility for you to—'

'You said you'd do it. Listen, Alan, don't try to squirm out of it. Barbara were here when you said it.'

'You can leave my secretary out of it!' Turner flared. He was touched on the raw by the thought that, if it came to a crunch, Barbara would probably support Joe against him. 'And let me tell you, you've a funny idea of the scope of your duties if you don't understand that you have to check every detail yourself.'

Joe was speechless.

'What's more, I don't like your attitude over this. Instead of doing what you could to make good your omissions, you're trying to shove the blame off. Well, it won't do! You've half an hour before knocking off time – use it to work out how we're going to make good the unnecessary expense you've put us to today.'

There was a moment when Turner was in danger of being seized by the lapels of his jacket and dragged over the desk by Joe. But the phone rang, Turner picked it up, and Joe walked out without actually laying hands on him.

Next morning Turner, who was in a state of great inner

76

anxiety, received a further blow. Frank Dinsdale came to the estate office and threw his weight about. 'Listen, when I came and fetched them cattle for you yesterday, I were doing you a favour.'

'Yes, and charged us double rates to prove it!'

'Aye, well, think on! There's more to come on top of that bill.'

'What?' Turner cried, outraged. 'I thought it was way over the top when I found it on my desk this morning, but if you think you're adding anything—'

'Hold on, hold on. I'm not putting my rates up any further. But fair's fair. It were your fault I got done.'

Turner's heart sank. He had no idea what was coming but he could tell it was bad news.

'Well, go on.'

'You know you wouldn't let me spend time putting up them partitions?'

'I told you we were in a hurry, yes.'

'Hey up, lad! Your cattleman Billy checked with you 'cos he thought I ought to put 'em up, and you told him no.'

'Well, what of it?'

'Only that RSPCA inspector may prosecute. And let me tell you, I don't intend to pay a fine for summat as isn't my fault.'

'What RSPCA inspector?'

'Ted Baynes. And he's a tough one. If I get took to court, I shall have to plead guilty and pay up – and the money's not coming out of *my* pocket.'

'Look here, any fines you incur—'

'Were your fault. Don't try to wriggle off the hook, Mr Turner. If you don't agree to pay my fine, I'll plead not guilty and tell the magistrate you ordered me not to put in my partitioning.'

With that Dinsdale smiled in triumph and left. He knew – and so did Turner – that the last thing NY Estates wanted was to be named in court as contributing to the discomfort of livestock. He knew that by the time he got back to his scrappy little office in Hotten, Turner would be on the telephone offering soothing syrup.

Joe hadn't come to the office to give his usual mid-morning report. He was taking care to stay out of Turner's way that morning, for fear that if they encountered one another they'd have a stand-up fight. He was out the far side of NY's land, looking at the field on which the cattle would have to be pastured until the next convenient sale.

His brother Jack drove up at about eleven. 'Hey, Joe!' Joe walked over to the Land Rover. 'Yes?'

'Billy told me you were out here. I wanted a word.'

'About what?'

Jack surveyed him. His brother's tone of voice was sharp, his manner curt. Perhaps this wasn't the moment . . .

'What is it, Jack? If it's about that daft nannygoat, my advice is to get rid of it.'

'Nay, it's summat different. Joe, what did you say to Ma yesterday that upset her so much?'

Joe stared at him. Jack could see he was genuinely surprised, the usually goodnatured face creased in a frown. 'Perhaps you'd better ask Ma that.'

'I did, and she skirted round the answer. Look, Joe, if it was about this business between you and Barbara Peters—'

'What business?' Joe broke in with so much ferocity that Jack drew his arm away from the window of the Land Rover.

'Nay, now . . . Don't jump at me like that, Joe. You must know everybody in Beckindale's talking about it. Seth was on at me in the Woolpack last night.'

'Oh, Seth!'

'It's not just him, lad. Henry Wilks helped me choke him off last night but when I said the story was a load of rubbish he shook his head and looked worried.'

'I'm right sorry to have worried Henry Wilks,' Joe said in a cold tone. 'And Ma. It's very good of everybody to be so concerned about me.'

'Point is, Joe – have they reason to be?'

'What business is it of yours?'

'Well . . . ' Jack hesitated. 'Ma's upset. I don't like her to be upset.'

Joe sighed. 'Look, Jack, she asked me if there were owt between me and Barbara, I told her no, and she said she believed me.'

'But in that case . . . ?'

'In that case, there ought to be an end of it, eh? But now we get this nonsense about harming Mr Hinton. Hang it, what does she want? I can't *not* talk to Barbara even if I wanted to – she's my boss's secretary.'

'I realize that. but there's this tale of her staying all night at your cottage.'

'And it's quite true. She slept in the spare room. And why? Because she didn't want to go home and face a lecture from her father.' As he saw Jack look a little incredulous at the story, Joe drew in a breath of impatience. 'You know, a man and a woman don't have to jump into bed together just because they're alone under the same roof! What she needed that night was time to get herself together after a bruising encounter with that husband of hers.'

'I see.'

'Do you? Ma says I'm coming between Barbara and this Brian she's wed to.'

'And you're not?'

Joe took a moment to reply. He wanted to be honest. 'I don't think I'm breaking up their marriage—'

'But are you hindering their reconciliation?'

'How the devil do I know?' Joe exclaimed. 'All I know is, if I send her to coventry, she'll have not a single soul in this benighted village that she can turn to.'

'I think Ma wants her to turn to her father.'

'What Ma wants has nowt to do with it, Jack. If there was a real relationship between Hinton and his daughter, she wouldn't have to be driven by loneliness to confide in him. I'm not blaming t'vicar – he has views, Barbara has hers. But he shouldn't expect her to live by his commandments.'

'The ones he lives by are in the Bible, lad. Heavy, they are.'

'Yeah, full of Thou-shalt-nots. But what about the Thou-shalts? Thou shalt understand, Thou shalt listen, Thou shalt be a friend—'

'Is that it then, Joe? You're doing a bit of the Thou-shalts?'

In all honesty, Joe had to admit he'd never thought it out this far before. 'All I know is, I like Barbara. I'm not stopping, just because it makes other folk uneasy.'

Jack shook his head in silent consideration. Then he let in the clutch and prepared to drive off. 'Trouble is,' he said with a wry smile, 'people like Seth just don't think like that.'

At lunchtime Joe went to the Woolpack for a snack. There he met, of all people, Barbara Peters and her husband, Brian. It was the first time he'd encountered the husband who figured in Barbara's problems.

'Brian, this is Joe Sugden, the farm manager at NY,' Barbara introduced.

The two men shook hands. Joe took against him immediately because of the proprietary way he held on to Barbara's elbow.

'How d'you like Beckindale?' he inquired, to make conversation.

'It has its points, I suppose.'

'Staying long?'

Brian Peters had come to Beckindale because he had an insurance inquiry in the neighbourhood. It seemed a good opportunity to make another attempt at softening his wife's resistance, simply by making a little side excursion.

But it was she who answered Joe. 'Brian will be driving back tonight.'

So that put paid to that. He was irritated. Hang it, he wasn't used to having to put in so much work to persuade a woman to change her mind. He wasn't exactly a ladies' man, but he had a way with women when he wanted. But though he wanted it to work on Barbara, it was having almost the opposite effect. The more he tried to charm her, the more she retreated.

He took her to a good restaurant for lunch – one more attempt at the classic softening-up. They were very civilized, very calm. They talked about the weather, the countryside, the christening due to take place the following Sunday in St Mary's.

Only as the waiter came to offer liqueurs did Brian turn to what he wanted to say. 'D'you really want me to go home tonight?'

'Yes.'

'All right then. Come with me.'

'No.'

'But why not? It's easy to see there's nothing to hold you here! Country christening, trouble with a transporter – it sounds like Dullsville.'

'Perhaps it is.'

'Then why . . . ?'

'If I leave here, Brian, it won't be to come to you.'

She said it in an even, unemphatic tone which carried all the more conviction because she didn't raise her voice.

'Barbara!' he protested.

'I don't know why you won't accept it. It's not even as if you love me all that much. It's just . . . more convenient if we patch it up.'

'Oh, it's more than that—'

'Not much, love,' she said gently. 'Come on, pay the bill and drive me back. My boss will be wondering where I've got to.'

'And that's another thing!' he put in. 'By all I can hear of him, he's a right little toe-rag! Why on earth are you working for him?'

'Because it's the only game in town.'

'There you are! If you came back—'

'If I want a better job I can move on elsewhere. When I'm ready.'

'Is that it? You just need more time?'

She sighed, got up, and signalled to the waiter that she wanted her coat. Brian paid the bill and escorted her to his car. Little wheels were going round in his mind. All he had to do was play it out – she needed more time, she'd come round in the end.

He dropped her at Home Farm. 'I'll be back home by seven tonight,' he said. 'I'm there if you need me – tonight and most nights.'

'Yes, thank you, Brian. Thank you for a lovely lunch.'

He was too exasperated by her childlike good manners than do more than wave at her and drive off. Turner, having watched it all through the window, was rather pleased. It certainly seemed they weren't on lovey-dovey terms yet.

'Had a good lunch?' he inquired with great affability as she came in.

She'd been expecting complaints for a two hours' absence. 'Excellent food,' she said.

'Where did you go? Chelbey Manor? Those people who've taken it over are really first class.' He chatted on about various good meals he'd had at the restaurant. He was just about to end by inviting her to dinner there some evening in the near future when he realized he had lost her attention. She was deep in study of a page of figures she had to collate.

Turner was vexed. It wasn't just that she played hard to get. She didn't play at all. She simply wasn't interested in him. Hard though it was to accept, he had to believe she didn't want his attentions.

In fact, for some strange reason, she seemed to prefer Joe Sugden.

Barbara had a dire evening with her father. He, good man, was eager to know if Brian's unexpected visit had touched her heart. He saw it as a good mark for Brian that he should be willing to drive up here, out of his way, just to spend an hour or two with her. It *must* make her feel a little indebted.

But in fact that was just what she resented. Why couldn't they believe her when she said she needed to be left alone?

Still, there was no reason to take out her resentment against her father, who meant well. She cooked dinner for them both, spending as long as she could in the kitchen, but by eight o'clock there was nothing to do but sit down with him to eat.

Donald Hinton made himself refrain from asking outright what she and her husband had talked about. But he edged round it for so long that in the end she said: 'I tried to make Brian see that I don't want him popping up here at odd moments. It's better if he doesn't.'

'But you have to keep in touch with him, my dear.'

'There's always the telephone.'

'Have you arranged to ring him, then?'

'He says he'll be home most evenings.'

'Yes, but are you—' He broke off. He could see her colour rising. 'I'm sorry,' he said.

'That's what you keep saying! You keep walking in on my private affairs and then when I let you see I don't like it, you think it's mended if you say, "Sorry".'

'But it's only natural that I—'

'There's coffee in the percolator,' she said. 'I'm going out.'

'Barbara! At this hour?'

'Good heavens, it's only a quarter to nine!'

Of course. In a town, it was still the early evening. But here in the country, where the darkness was so entire except in the village centre, people didn't just pop out in the middle of the evening.

'Where are you going?'

'I don't know. For a drive. To the Woolpack. I don't know.'

She went out. He had the sense not to follow her into the hall arguing. He heard her drive away. He stood behind the closed front door, feeling a total failure as a priest, a father, and a man.

Barbara had really nowhere to go. She didn't want to go alone to the Woolpack; though its clientele were polite enough, they still regarded her as a novelty. And moreover, an oddity – a vicar's daughter, separated from her legal husband, turning up in a pub on her own . . . ?

83

The country roads were no fun to drive in at night. Her headlights kept throwing up scurrying creatures in her path. After about fifteen minutes she headed back to Beckindale.

The only place left to go to was Joe's cottage.

He showed her in after a surprised exclamation. The table in his sitting room was covered with papers and pamphlets to do with farming, and so were most of the chairs. He cleared a space for her on the sofa.

'Well,' he said, studying her, 'what d'you need? Coffee or a stiff brandy?'

'Neither. I just need . . . not to be talked at.'

'Can do. I'm in the middle of summat. You sit there and contemplate eternity while I get to a point where I can stop.'

Without more ado he sat down to the table and immersed himself in his work. She curled her legs under her on the sofa, relaxing against its back. At first her mind whirled on – Brian, her father, her future, her marriage. But after a time she found she was studying Joe's profile.

He had a nice profile. Slightly untidy dark hair, a snubbish nose, a firm chin. His hands were capable and purposeful when he reached out to pick up a paper. His clothes were a lot below Brian's standards – rather rumpled check shirt, sleeveless pullover, shapeless cords.

'Well?' he said, looking up suddenly.

'Oh!'

'Caught you at it! Don't you know us country types can sense when we're being watched? It comes of being close to nature, you see.'

'I'm sorry. I was just . . . '

'Ready to talk yet?'

'There seems nothing more to say, Joe. Brian seems such a stranger. I sat opposite him at lunch today, talking about the crops, and wondered why on earth I was bothering.'

'I understand that. You've changed completely. What seems less clear is how he feels.'

'He feels that his life has been unnecessarily complicated

by the lack of a wife.' Tears began to trickle over the rims of her eyes. 'Do you know, Joe, he's never once said, "I love you and miss you".'

'Happen he's not too good at expressing—'

'Oh, he can do it if he wants to!' she cried. A great sob overtook her. She searched for a handkerchief, covered her face with it, and gave herself up to her tears.

After a bit she felt Joe beside her on the sofa. He put an arm about her. 'Come on, lass,' he said. He drew her against him so that her head rested against his shoulder. He was treating her as he would have a frightened puppy or a lamb.

When the sobs had died away, she straightened. 'I'm sorry.'

'Don't apologize.'

'That's what I keep saying to Daddy.' She produced a watery smile. 'But it's worse for you. All this is nothing to do with you.'

'That might be true except that we seem to have a lot in common.'

'Did you feel as bad as I do, when you and your wife broke up?'

'Reckon so. But you get over it. If folk will only leave you alone—'

'Oh, if only they would!'

'That's difficult hereabouts. Beckindalers love to gossip.' He hesitated. 'My mother had a word about that. She . . . she was worried.'

'Because I stayed here overnight?'

He nodded.

'I'm sorry if I made it difficult for you.'

'Oh, you don't want to worry about that. I'm used to being in the thick of the local tongue-wagging.'

'Do you lead such a scandalous life, then?'

'Listen, love, if there were a gossip column in t'*Hotten Courier*, I'd be a godsend to it.'

She laughed, and he did too. But after a moment they found themselves studying each other with serious attention.

85

'It's so good, being with you, Joe.'

'Yes.'

'I feel . . . valued.'

'Yes.'

'Joe, I don't want to leave.'

He drew her close to him again. She kissed him gently on the cheek.

'I suppose we're justifying all the gossip,' she murmured with a hidden smile.

'I don't know why you have to keep on talking so much,' Joe said, and kissed her with a sudden passion that put an end to all the talk.

Chapter Seven

The following Sunday, the christening of young Samuel David Skilbeck took place. Joe, blushing inwardly a little at his recent sins of the flesh, was one of the godfathers. Barbara had been invited to the christening lunch; Annie issued the invitation, firmly disregarding any embarrassment it might cause.

To allow the womenfolk time to get the meal on the table, Joe took Barbara to the Woolpack for a pre-lunch drink. Henry Wilks was surprised to see them. 'Aren't you going up to Emmerdale, Joe?'

'Later, later – when all the fetching and carrying's been done.' Joe grinned. 'You forget, I know what it's like there when we're expecting company.'

Alan Turner was standing at the bar drinking a fine malt whisky. 'Good morning, Barbara,' he said in a very cool tone.

She refused to be put off by the ice in his manner. 'Were you in church for the christening?'

'Not I. An estate manager's time isn't his own. Especially when he has to pick up the pieces after other people.' This was said without a glance at Joe, but his meaning was quite apparent.

Heck, thought Joe, let's try a little Christian peace-making; after all, I've just been in church promising to guide that scrap on the right road. 'Let me fill that up for you,' he said, with a gesture at Turner's glass.

Barbara laughed. 'He's in a godly frame of mind. He's a godfather.'

'Is he indeed? Well, he can start living up to the principles by sorting out some of the problems he's caused.' He turned sharply to Joe. 'I had a visit from an RSPCA inspector last thing yesterday.'

'Oh.'

'You never mentioned any of that to me when you left the bill for Dinsdale's services on my desk.'

Amos came down the bar with Joe's drinks. 'There you are, Joe, that'll be one pound, eight pence.'

'And another thing,' Turner surged on, raising his voice over Amos' remark, 'I don't like this business of leaving messages on my desk. I expect verbal reports—'

'Mr Turner,' began Amos, in a placating tone, 'please let's have no unpleasantness—'

'Let's leave it till tomorrow, Alan,' Joe said, keeping his temper. 'This isn't the time or place.'

'I'll say when it's the time and place.'

'Alan!' Barbara said, coming between the two men. She laid a hand on his sleeve. 'Alan, this is no way to behave.'

He was stopped short. He went red, tried to form words to gainsay her criticism.

'You shouldn't be airing NY problems in a public place,' she murmured.

'No . . . no, perhaps not.' She had given him a gentle warning that he was making a fool of himself in front of an audience.

'I think you need a holiday, you know. Why don't you arrange for a few days off?'

It was not meant ironically, but it had its ironic under-tones – for if any man was adept at swanning off when he wanted to, it was Alan Turner. All the same, he seized the excuse. 'Pressure of responsibility,' he muttered, and knocking back the remains of his drink, hurried out.

Half an hour later, in a good mood that Turner hadn't been able to spoil, Joe drove Barbara to the christening lunch.

The kitchen-living room of the Old Barn was under pressure to accommodate all the guests. But the weather was mild, the kitchen door stood open, people could stroll out into the April air.

Seth Armstrong had managed to inveigle himself into the group, coming as an appendage of Jackie Merrick. He was already a little tight; after his usual two pints, he had downed a couple of whiskies in the Woolpack cadged from Henry in honour of the christening. When the sparkling wine was opened for a toast to the baby, Seth naturally made sure he got more than his share. So his tongue was even looser than usual when he found himself alongside Dolly's aunt from Darlington, Aunt Jessie.

'Happen we'll soon have summat else to cel-celebrate,' he hiccuped.

'Oh? Somebody else with a baby to christen?'

'Nay, a wedding, a wedding.' He gave her an enormous wink. 'Joe's heading for church, I reckon – at least not church, 'cos he's divorced. And so'll she be, of course.'

'Who?' said Aunt Jessie, mystified. She'd heard nothing of Annie's younger son having a girlfriend. But then she'd only arrived Saturday morning.

'Her – there,' Seth said, nodding, and then regretting it because his head was already beginning to hurt.

Aunt Jessie looked at the pretty girl in pale blue helping herself to cold turkey and salad at the buffet table. 'Yon's a pretty lass!'

'Aye, t'vicar's daughter.'

She looked dubious. 'Are you sure, Seth? A vicar's daughter, but divorced?'

'Nay, she's not divorced *yet* – but it's coming, I'll guarantee you that. 'Cos she's thrown her bonnet over t'windmill wi' our Joe.'

Aunt Jessie laughed. 'Oh, Seth,' she said, digging him in the ribs with her elbow. She was used to his tall tales, which she'd heard on previous visits.

'Nay, I mean it. Her car's been parked outside Joe's place overnight twice this week – I see that, y'know, I'm a gamekeeper, have to be out and about at all hours in pur-pursuance of me duties.'

Aunt Jessie wasn't shocked. She had long ago come to terms with the overthrow of old conventions. She looked at Barbara and decided Joe had made a good choice.

This being her view, she had no hesitation in saying so

to Annie Sugden when the ebb and flow of movement brought them together.

'Barbara?' Annie said. 'I think you've got a wrong impression, Jessie. There's no talk of a marriage between them. In any case, Barbara's already married.'

'So I hear, but that's just a matter of waiting for the divorce, I gather.'

Annie frowned. 'There's no talk of a divorce.'

'Oh . . . I'm sorry, I thought it were more or less serious, since she's stayed overnight wi' him.'

Annie frowned. So far as she knew, there had only been one occasion. It seemed odd that anyone would bother to relate that to Jessie, since it was somewhat in the past now.

'Who told you that?'

'Who else but Seth! He knows all that goes on, doesn't he? We've just been having a chat. I said to him, Just because a girl's car is parked outside a feller's house on a couple of nights, that's no proof. But he says a neighbour told him he was right – he likes to check his facts,' Jessie laughed.

She had no idea of the wound she was inflicting.

'Excuse me,' said Annie. She left Jessie rather abruptly, to thread her way to the table where Joe was just heaping his plate.

'Joe, I need to speak to you.'

'Hang on till I get this food—'

'Leave that. Leave it, Joe.'

He looked fully at her. Her expression told him it was serious. 'We'd best go outside,' he said.

He elbowed a path for them to the fresh air of the farmyard. Daffodils and narcissus were in full bloom in the tubs, scenting the air under the spring sun. Annie paid no heed to them. She wheeled and faced her son.

'How could you, Joe?'

'Just a minute, Ma—' He had no doubt what she meant. Only one thing could cause her to use that tone of deep reproach.

'After what we discussed—'

90

'It didn't happen like that. You don't understand.'

'What is there to understand? I asked you to show some thought for others.'

'I never heard you asking me to show some thought for Barbara!'

'This doesn't help Barbara, this news I've had—'

'Oh, I might have known it would get twisted by the gossips!'

'Are you saying it's not so? Are you saying she spent two more nights in your spare room?'

'No, I'm not claiming that.'

'I think you'd better leave, Joe.'

'Ma—'

'I want you to leave.'

It was the first time in his life he'd ever been ordered away from Emmerdale. He was stricken to silence. His mother turned and walked back into the Skilbeck house, where her duties lay. Joe stood a long moment staring at the doorway through which she had disappeared, then went to fetch Barbara to take her home.

En route he told her what had happened. She caught her breath. 'I suppose it was bound to become common knowledge. You warned me of that, Joe.'

'I'd like to lay my hands on the person that chewed it all over and spat it out to my mother!'

'It doesn't matter who's responsible. The fact is, I'll have to speak to my father now – before some kind friend tells him.'

'Aw, Barbara . . . ' He knew how much she dreaded that. 'Would you like me to—'

'What? Defend my honour to him? It's hardly possible, is it? No, leave it with me, Joe.'

She stayed indoors waiting for the vicar to return from the christening party. He arrived looking pleased and relaxed, unusually so for him. Everyone at Emmerdale always made him feel at ease.

But one look at his daughter's face told him there was trouble coming. She always looked pale and tense when she had something important to say.

He tried to ease her into it. 'You and Joe left the party rather abruptly, my dear. Is anything wrong?'

'Mrs Sugden asked Joe to go.'

'What?' Hinton was truly startled. Annie's love for her sons was one of the mainstays of her life. She must have been deeply angered or hurt to turn one of them away.

'She'd heard . . . something . . . '

'About you and Joe?'

She nodded. 'Why can't people just leave things alone?' she burst out, her dark grey eyes flashing with indignation. 'Joe and I have a lot in common and so we . . . we turn to each other. But it's nothing to do with anyone else.'

After a moment's hesitation her father said: 'It's to do with Brian, perhaps.'

'How does it concern him? I left him weeks ago.'

'But unfaithfulness – and we are talking about unfaithfulness, are we not—?'

She laughed in contempt. 'Unfaithfulness! How can you be "faithful" to a marriage that's over?'

He shook his head. 'To me that term is meaningless. A marriage can never be over – you know that's my belief.'

'Yes, and that's why I had to speak to you before someone else did. Joe and I are . . . I suppose you could call it "involved". I can't tell you how seriously as yet.'

He looked grieved by her words. 'Barbara, have you given any consideration to Joe's part in all this? Involved! Does he understand what that means, coming between man and wife?'

'Oh, I've explained over and over again! No one is coming between me and Brian! Not even the girl he's been sleeping with – it was all at an end before that, I realize it now. We don't mean anything to each other any more.'

'That's your view now, while you're still hurt and confused . . . '

'I'm not confused! I wish you'd stop reading things into

my words that I don't mean. I'm quite clear-headed, I don't want to take up with Brian again, my marriage is a thing of the past.'

'And . . . is Joe your future?'

'Oh, good heavens, we haven't thought about anything like that!'

'I see. You just rush in, without a thought for what it means.'

'I don't know that we "rushed".'

'Don't you think you're being rather selfish?'

'What?' He had taken her by surprise.

'Looking at it purely from my own standpoint – have you ever thought of the position I'm placed in by your behaviour?'

'Oh, Daddy . . . '

'This morning I performed a christening ceremony and used the occasion to call my flock to renew their vows to God. What will they think when they see that my words are wasted on my own daughter?'

He had effectively put an end to the discussion. She couldn't reply to a question like that. Her view was that she had no responsibility to her father's parishioners – they had their life to lead and she had hers. They had no cause to look to her for an example just because she happened to be born the daughter of a churchman.

She went up to her room to think things over. Maybe it would be easier if she left the vicarage. It would certainly spare her these conversations which could only end in hurt on either side.

But where could she go?

She could always move in with Joe, of course – she was sure he would welcome her. But that was too definite a commitment. As yet she wasn't ready to partner herself with another man. She had just walked away from one mistake, she had no intention of walking straight into another.

Hinton sat thinking long after Barbara had left the room. He felt he ought to talk the matter over with Annie Sugden.

She had influence with Joe, he was sure of that. Perhaps she could speak to the boy . . . And yet, clearly, she already had, since it seemed they had quarrelled earlier.

He would seek her out next day. He had parish business to discuss with her, in any case.

The next day started badly at Emmerdale. The postman brought a bank statement which Jack read without comment. He took it out to show Matt, who was clearing up in the mistle, but Matt only nodded and handed it back.

Jack sighed inwardly. Matt was a wonderful helper in many ways, but when it came to the business side he had no views. He didn't understand finance and didn't pretend to.

He tucked the statement into his jacket pocket then went to Hotten on business. When he came home, elevenses was over and Donald Hinton was just leaving. Jack thought his mother looked rather sad.

He was right. She and the vicar had had a conversation ending in the conclusion that there was nothing to be done about the two young people. 'They don't think they're doing owt wrong, you see, vicar,' Annie had sighed as he took his leave. 'That's where it all breaks down – it's no use appealing to their conscience, they don't see it the way we do.'

Thus Jack could scarcely have chosen a worse moment to broach the subject that was on his mind. It had to be done, however. 'Ma, I think you ought to take a look at this,' he said. He produced the bank statement.

She scanned it. 'My word,' she said in a low voice. 'That's not very good . . . '

'That's an understatement,' Jack said, and then laughed despite himself at the pun.

'Where does the money go, lad? It just seems to be running out of the account like water!'

'I'll have to go through the accounts line by line, Ma. I've got to find the leak and plug it.'

'You could speak to Harold Dukes. He's seen us through before.'

94

'I've just tried that,' Jack said with a rueful grin. 'While I was in Hotten I dropped in on our bank manager. He wants to be helpful, Ma – but he pointed out he's had a lot of calls on his goodwill these last few months. We're not the only milk producers who're having a hard time with these new regulations.'

There were several things coming uppermost in Annie's mind. There was the cheap feed they'd bought a few months ago which proved to have some waste products in it, resulting in a sudden reduction in milk yield and some sickness among the herd. After that there had been vet's bills.

Then there had been the buying of some heifers which had proved to be a bad bargain. And there was the goat, which Pat had bought without consultation at a very high price. The goat was a source of complaint from everyone – it had got loose half a dozen times, brought down Dolly's washline, eaten some of Sam's newly washed underwear, munched the tulips in the tubs, and had a healthy appetite for animal feed besides.

She didn't want to mention all that to Jack. His shortcomings as a farmer were one of her great worries but she was always aware that he could get fed up and leave home again, just as easily as he did the first time. She didn't want to lose him despite all the problems he had brought with him – especially as her grandson Jackie was settling down to life at Emmerdale and making a go of his new job in Hotten.

She and her son talked round the problem for a time, she wary in case she implied blame to him, he apparently unaware of the seriousness of his mistakes. In the end she said, 'I'll talk to Henry about it. He's the man with the head for figures.'

While Joe had been manager of the farm, Henry and he had kept in close contact over the finances. But Jack somewhat distrusted Henry, thought him 'hard' over some decisions. For a moment it looked as if he would protest now, but he ended by shrugging. 'All right, I suppose he's the one who might see a way through this.'

Annie telephoned an invitation to Henry to come for a serious discussion after the Woolpack had closed for the afternoon. He arrived looking expectant. To tell the truth, he thought it was going to be about Joe, whose misdoings were being openly talked of in the bar by the locals.

'Sit thee down, lad, I've got the tea made,' Annie said in her usual hospitable fashion. 'I expect you'd like a bit of parkin?'

'No thanks, Annie. Much though I enjoy your baking, I'm trying to get my waistline down. Tea'll do me.' He accepted his cup, sipped, then said: 'Well?'

'I want you to look at this, Henry.' She passed him the bank statement.

He laid it on the kitchen table to read while he drank his tea. All at once he frowned, set his cup aside, and picked up the sheet. 'Hey-up,' he said.

'It's bad, isn't it?'

'It's certainly not good. Have you checked this?'

'Well, that's not up to me, lad. That's Jack's department. He said he'd go through the accounts and see.'

'You mean he doesn't know whether or not he's over-spending without having an accounting?'

She was silent.

'Annie,' Henry said, 'do you know Emmerdale Farm Limited is heading for the bankruptcy court?'

Chapter Eight

The shock of Henry's words made Annie catch her breath. Recently she'd been worried by signs of slackness about the farm, but she had told herself not to be critical. Her son Jack was a newly married man with many problems to solve – she mustn't expect him to give the same minute attention to every farming routine that Joe did.

'Where's the statement before this one?' Henry inquired.

'Jack keeps 'em in the parlour sideboard. But it's locked and he has the key – at least, I don't know where it is.'

Henry grunted in dissatisfaction. 'Will you ask him to let me have it, and the bills that go with it, and with this statement – and the returned cheques too, please.'

She was about to say, that's like an inquisition, isn't it? But then she remembered that dire word – bankruptcy.

'I expect we got them,' she said. 'But whether Jack actually kept them . . . '

'Anybody running a one-man business ought to—'

'But I don't think of Emmerdale as a one-man business, Henry!' she cried. 'You're the business head among us – now that Joe's gone, none of us have the experience.'

Henry sat back and looked rather grim.

'It's like this, lad,' she went on, anxious to make a new beginning as soon as possible. 'You used to take a lot more hand in the running of the business side. When Joe were in charge, you and him were always having little conferences. I dunno how it is but recently . . . '

He nodded. 'I haven't wanted to interfere too much now Jack's taken over. He has his views, you know.'

'Yes, I know. But after all, we *have* to make a profit. You're the one that knows the ins and outs of that sort of thing.'

'But I took it for granted that you were muddling through somehow—' He broke off, sorry for the word 'muddling'. But in truth that's how he saw Jack's efforts as a farmer.

He looked back over the past year or so and understood that he had been far too fainthearted. He had given in over the buying of Hathersage's land, he had in fact even helped to finance it, just so that Jack would stay on the place. But that had been a mistake.

The Hathersage acres, farmed without the use of chemicals or modern intensification, were a tremendous drain on the finances of Emmerdale. Much of Hathersage was lying fallow, no help to the production of pasture or animal feed. Moreover, Jack spent a lot of his time and energy on it instead of concentrating on what was important – the profit-making of the main farm.

There had been some very bad pieces of management recently, the buying of poor quality feed and a disaster over two 'cheap' heifers. There had been the crisis over Matt wanting to leave, and the necessity to invest money in turning the Old Barn into a proper home for him and his wife.

As a recent example of folly, Jack had not prevented his wife from buying that idiotic goat – and what was worse, he hadn't insisted on having it sold now that its nuisance value had been amply demonstrated. A goat! What possible use was it on a dairy farm? He had heard Pat murmuring that it would be good to buy a billy and breed from Annabelle, but now that he was being asked to take charge, he'd soon put a stop to that.

But first he had to be sure that Annie was speaking for Jack too when she hinted that Henry ought to take more part.

'Are you sure you want me to go into this?' he asked, waving the bank statement.

'I want things put on an even keel, Henry.'

'And Jack? What will Jack say?'

'He'll be glad to be rid of the responsibility,' she said, acknowledging at last a simple truth – that her son only

98

liked the contact with the land and nature, not the business of farming.

'Well, if I took it on, I'd want complete control,' Henry said, to make sure she understood the situation. 'I'd want all the bills and invoices as they come in, and I'd want to sign all the cheques before anything was paid, and I'd expect to be consulted before anything was bought other than run-of-the-mill items.'

'Aye, I understand that.'

'But will the lads understand it?' he urged. 'Joe, perhaps – he's a head on his shoulders, he'll see there's no other way to run it. But Matt and Jack?'

'You leave them to me, Henry.'

'You'll have to explain that if I take on the responsibility, I expect to have the authority too. Sitha, lass – they might not feel too happy if they have to see me every time they want to spend money. It's great having someone take on the bills, but when you want to buy fancy new equipment—'

'Matt never wants to do owt like that except for his sheep, and he's not likely to expect anything again for a while, now he's got his lambing shelters. As to Jack . . . '

'Aye, as to Jack. What when he comes to me saying he needs a special plough for Hathersage because the ordinary one isn't suitable? What when he wants to build an extension on the house for Jackie to have a place of his own?'

'Aye.' She was silent for a while. Jack was not easy to argue with when he got an idea in his head. It had been touch-and-go over the Old Barn – Jack had dearly wanted that for Pat and himself.

As she thought about it all, she realized that ever since Jack took over from Joe, there had been nothing but outlay at Emmerdale. At first Jack's earnings as a bestselling writer had financed that, but he had had no idea how much he had in the bank. And when it came to the point, he found – so she afterwards learned – that he'd forgotten he had an Income Tax bill to settle.

So the long and short of it was that though occasional small sums still came in from Jack's literary efforts and the film that was made from his book, there was really nothing but the income from the farm. And for almost two years they had been living far beyond that income.

She knew that, even if it meant a stand-up fight with Jack, she had to get it across to him that their finances must be handed over to Henry. 'I'll talk it all over with him,' she said. 'Don't you fret, lad, I'll sort it with our Jack.'

'Right. I'll come back first thing in the morning. Tell Jack I'll want all papers relative to Emmerdale Farm Limited.' He glanced about. 'I don't suppose there's anywhere I could use as an office?'

'Only the parlour.'

He thought about the Emmerdale parlour – full of best furniture, only used for great occasions such as wedding breakfasts or funeral gatherings. 'Nay . . . I'd best take it all down the Woolpack and operate from there.' That would be best, really. It would make a distance between himself and Jack which might be quite advantageous. When Jack was struck by an idea for which he needed money, it would give him time to think it over if he had to come indoors and ring Henry before he could get moving on it.

Annie made no objection to his plan. He rose to take his leave. 'Tell Jack I'll need all the correspondence from now on – he's not to poke letters behind the clock and forget 'em.' His glance there showed two, opened and rather crumpled. Annie smiled and sighed.

As Henry walked back to the village, his mind was busy. He blamed himself. He should have spoken up sooner. No need to let Annie be scared and upset like this. But then you'd think that Jack would have more sense . . .

It wasn't as if he didn't have a good example always before his eyes. There was NY Estates, where despite the slack grip of Alan Turner everything worked well and a good profit was made – chiefly because Joe never let things slide.

Of course Henry didn't expect Jack to work Emmerdale in the same way as NY worked their land. In the first place he didn't have the funds or the scope, and in the second place he actively disapproved of 'agri-business'. Yet you'd have thought that he'd learn order and application simply from watching the work on NY's fields.

Well, happen it wasn't too late. Henry would do his best to bring Emmerdale back into the black, even if he had to make himself unpopular to do so.

At that moment Alan Turner was feeling less approving of NY Estates and its methods. He'd just had the rough side of Mr Lattimore's tongue.

When he got back from a rather expansive lunch with an equipment supplier in Hotten, he found a note on his blotter from Barbara: HQ rang, wish to speak to you urgently, please return call.

He dialled the number and was put through. 'Good afternoon, Mr Lattimore, Turner here at Beckindale—'

'Oh, so there you are,' came Lattimore's voice, very cool. 'Where have you been all day? My secretary's tried four times to get you.'

'Oh . . . er . . . I had some things to look over at Grey Top, and then an appointment in Hotten about the new harrow—'

'Well, now you're there – what does this mean, this extraordinary report that our stock was returned from the market because prices were too low?'

'Well, they were, sir – offers were about ten per cent under what—'

'I have a report here on Hotten Market prices on that day, Turner. Prices began at a very healthy level for beef cattle.'

'Yes, well, if you read on, Mr Lattimore, you'll see that—'

'Yes, I see that a complete mess was made of transporting the beasts to Hotten. Who is this haulage firm, Dinsdale's? And why are we expected to pay their fine for incorrect transport of farmstock?'

'There was a breakdown on our transporter, sir – we had to get Dinsdale at the last moment. I must say, I thought his prices were extraordinary, but Sugden—'

'Sugden brought him in, yes, I see that. Because he was at market waiting to watch the sales?'

'Yes, that's right.'

'Why weren't you there?'

'I beg your pardon?'

'Why weren't you there? This was an important sale, our first offer of beef stores under our new beef-raising programme. First of all the arrangements don't seem suitable, and then when it comes to monitoring prices, you're not even there.'

'No . . . Well . . . You see . . . I had to rush off to Manchester . . . '

'Manchester?' repeated Lattimore in tones of disbelief and annoyance.

'Er . . . Yes . . . My wife, you know . . . There was a crisis . . . '

'What sort of crisis? Was she ill?'

'No . . . not exactly . . . er . . . She rang . . . She was upset . . . There had been a prowler in the block of flats,' said Turner, inventing wildly.

'Oh, I see.' Lattimore's tone became less irritated. You couldn't really criticize a man for rushing to the aid of his wife in a moment like that. 'She all right?'

'Oh . . . Yes, Mr Lattimore . . . I cheered her up . . . And as to the fine for the haulage firm, Dinsdale may not actually be prosecuted . . . '

'It doesn't matter. We must just write it off in the circumstances. What I really wanted to say, Turner, was about the pig unit.'

'The pig unit?' Turner said with a sinking heart. He knew nothing about it. It was Joe's idea completely, and because Turner hadn't taken the trouble to understand the profit-and-loss aspects – and moreover didn't like pigs – he always steered clear of it.

'This recent report on it is very surprising. Have you got the costs there for the heating of the farrowing house?'

'Er . . . no, sir . . . I'm afraid that's Joe's special responsibility, sir. I . . . er . . . can't quite . . . '

'Surely you can lay your hands on the figures?'

'I'm afraid not, Mr Lattimore. Joe . . . er . . . has his own ways . . . He's not trained in business methods, I'm afraid.'

'I see. Well, get him to ring me with the information, will you?'

'Yes, right away, Mr Lattimore.'

'No, I have a meeting now. Tell him first thing in the morning. It seems I have to talk to him personally if I want to know the details.'

'Yes, Mr Lattimore. First thing in the morning.'

Miserably aware that he'd made a bad showing, Turner put the phone down.

Next day Joe returned the call, with Turner eavesdropping shamelessly. He couldn't tell, from Joe's end of the conversation, whether he was getting a rocket or a slap on the back.

'Want to know more about it,' Joe said when he hung up. 'They're sending a couple of fellers to take a look.'

'Fellers?' cried Turner, unconsciously parroting Joe. 'What fellers? Who?'

'Dunno. Two of the directors.'

'Didn't he give the names?'

'No. What does it matter?'

It mattered a lot to Alan Turner. Some of the directors he knew and could handle, some he knew and *knew* he couldn't handle, and some were strangers – and therefore all the more dangerous.

'All we've got to do is show 'em the pig unit, whoever they are,' said Joe.

'If you think that, you prove that you know nothing about how business is done,' said Turner.

But Joe knew enough about business to be very concerned

103

when Henry Wilks showed him the Emmerdale books two days later.

'Heck, Henry, why didn't the accountants show us the danger?' he exclaimed.

Henry shrugged. 'We only have auditors every second year. This is one of the no-audit years.'

They were in Henry's room at the Woolpack. It was a capacious room, as befitted an old inn, but at the moment it was cluttered with papers arranged in neat piles on almost every surface, including the bed.

Henry had the main items on a little card table he'd brought down from the attic. He and Joe were seated at it, looking through the figures.

'The farm normally runs an overdraft,' Henry took it up, pointing to a list of items in his own handwriting. 'That's okay, most businesses work on the bank's money rather than their own. What went wrong here was – you remember that poor quality feed we got from Micklem's?'

'Oh, that!'

'Yes, that. Well, Jack entered into an arrangement to have it delivered regularly on a six months' contract. When it was found that the feed was below standard, Jack renewed the contract for the Prestige Mix – but forgot to cancel the other one.'

'You mean he's been paying for two lots of feed and only getting one?'

'Aye, lad.'

'For how long?'

'Six months.'

Joe groaned. As a shareholder of Emmerdale Farm Limited, he didn't expect to make a fortune, but he certainly didn't want to find himself in the bankruptcy court.

'It's this way, Joe. Jack clearly never looks at the invoices and bills. And he doesn't always pay 'em, either. He does bank the milk cheque regularly, I'll give him that, and on the whole he never lets money hang about if it comes in – he puts it straight into the account. But we've been going

104

steadily into the red over this double payment to Micklem's, and the bank were quite right to draw our attention to it.'

'They were an' all!'

'But even when we get back the money due from Micklem's, you can see that just brings us up to about even-stevens. It's not good, Joe. It's not good at all.'

Joe read his way through Henry's careful analysis of a year's income and output at Emmerdale. 'Expenses have gone up since Jack's marriage,' he murmured.

'Ye-es . . . we had to bear the cost of renovating the Old Barn, but that was a justified expense – we had to keep Matt with us. But apart from that, there's been furniture for the master bedroom and—'

'Henry, if we're not making enough to pay for justifiable expenses like that, it's a poor do!'

'Right, lad.' Henry ran a hand over his balding pate. 'Of course, now that Jackie's got a job, he'll not be on Emmerdale's payroll any more. And Tom Merrick is now responsible for Sandie's upkeep.'

'Aye, so all they need to do is prevent Pat buying a pedigree goat for two hundred and fifty quid and they can all be on the breadline!'

'I don't need to tell you that these new EEC regulations about milk production have had a severe effect. But to tell the truth, the downward slip at Emmerdale began long before those regulations came in. In a word, Joe, there's got to be a new broom at Emmerdale.'

'I'm with you. What we need is a board meeting to knock a few heads together.'

What he meant – and they both knew it – was that they had to impress Jack with the need for proper farming. No more buying a tractor just because a neighbour was prepared to sell it off cheap – if you had to go further into the overdraft to pay for it, the bank would get uneasy. No more farm animals bought as pets – goats were out from now on.

'We need an injection of cash, all the same,' Henry said.

'Managing from hand to mouth like this is bad business practice.'

'What d'you have in mind, Henry?'

'Well, we could get a mortgage on the farm—'

'You what? Jack'll go through the roof if you suggest that!'

'Well, suggest an alternative.'

Joe frowned. His mind was racing. 'Henry . . . How about . . . Let me think a minute . . .'

Henry watched him with interest. What was forming in that bright, efficient head?

'You'll recall that Emmerdale Farm Limited bought Demdyke for me when I was still farm manager?'

'Aye, and a good investment. I notice that your rent for Demdyke is one of the few things that appears regularly on the credit side!'

'Right. Well, what's it worth at today's prices?'

'Worth? Hey-up, Joe, you're not going to suggest we sell up Demdyke? The bank wouldn't like that. It's part of the collateral for our overdraft.'

'I'm not suggesting selling it away out of t'family. I were thinking . . . I'd like to buy it, Henry.'

At first Henry stared, and then understanding dawned. Of course! Demdyke would make a nice little home for a man if he were thinking of settling down. And clearly that was how Joe's thoughts were tending.

If Barbara Peters would agree . . .

Henry didn't pursue the thought aloud. He merely said: 'I'm calling a board meeting for next Saturday afternoon. If you're still of the same mind, you can raise it then.'

It was a matter that Joe would have to discuss with Barbara before he could be certain he wanted to go on with it. But everything was thrown into uncertainty by two events. First of all Turner was summoned to a headquarters conference at Lincoln and insisted on taking Barbara with him.

It meant an overnight stay. Joe was furious. 'You can't really mean you're going to fall for that?' he raged at

106

Barbara. 'I just don't believe it!'

'It's all on the level, Joe, really it is,' she soothed. 'I've talked on the phone myself with Mr Lattimore – there really is a conference, Turner really has to go, and he needs me with him.'

'Needs you!' sneered Joe.

She grew irritated. 'Listen, I've been out at work since I left commercial college. I'm a big girl. I know how to protect myself from anything that comes up—'

Joe pulled himself together. They were actually having their first quarrel – and over Alan Turner, of all people. 'Of course I accept that, Barbara.'

'And as it happens, I really do believe this is a straight business conference. We'll be in a hotel right under Lattimore's eyes. I don't think Alan would risk anything funny with the boss looking on.'

With that Joe had to be satisfied. But in the face of this danger and the disagreement it had caused between them, he felt a need to bind her all the closer to him.

'Listen, love, there's something I want to ask you. You like this cottage?'

'Of course.' She was surprised at the change of tack but, glancing about, nodded in satisfaction. 'Though I'm not entirely at one with your bachelor taste, it's a nice little place.'

'I'm thinking of buying it.'

'Buying it? I thought you already owned it?'

'Nay. It belongs to Emmerdale Farm Limited. And as they're a bit pushed for cash, I thought . . .'

She at first took it strictly on that level. 'Well, it's certainly a good investment. A nice little property – you could always sell at a profit.'

'I weren't thinking of it from that angle. I wondered, Barbara . . . if you'd think of it for us?'

That took her completely aback. She stared at him from her grey eyes, very alarmed.

'Oh, I don't think . . . '

'You and I make a good pair, Barbara. I thought—'

'I don't know that I want anything as definite as a – as a household.'

'Why not? This isn't just a passing thing with us, is it?'

He wanted her to reply at once: No, of course not. But honesty compelled her to take her time.

'I don't know, Joe. You're asking me for opinions I haven't formed as yet. All I know is that when I'm with you, I'm . . . I feel safe, guarded . . . But whether it's anything deeper, I don't know.'

'Listen, love—'

'It's too soon, Joe. I thought you understood that I don't want to rush into—'

'No, no, of course not. But if you'd think about it – about us having this place . . . '

He'd moved too fast. He had scared her. If anything, she drew back from him after that, and he cursed himself for being so heavy-handed.

All the same, he went to the board meeting with the firm intention of making an offer for Demdyke.

The gathering at Emmerdale was unusually nervous. Jack understood that decisions might be taken which he couldn't agree with, and which might reflect adversely on his management. Matt was worried because Dolly, hearing that the farm was in financial straits, had suggested the idea of a 'farm shop'. She had taken up butter-making and had sold some in Hotten at good prices. She also did spinning and weaving, which she proposed to sell; but it all sounded a lot of work for a new mother.

Annie was perturbed because she could see Jack was ready for a quarrel. She wanted above all to preserve the peace. But she didn't want to see Emmerdale go under the hammer. She wanted it preserved, entire, so that her grandson could inherit.

Joe was worried on a purely financial basis. He could sense Jack's intended opposition to any 'rationalization' of farming methods but he knew, from his experience with NY Estates, that only good management could keep a farm going these days. Everything seemed to be against dairy farming: public taste was turning against butter and cream and even rich milk, beef was only wanted if it was lean, and even Matt's sheep – prize-winners though they were – brought more for their wool than for their meat.

Henry called them to order, then began on the financial status. He had cleared up the problem of the bank statement, been in touch with Micklem's and was assured a cheque would be with him within a few days. Everyone carefully avoided looking at Jack as this mistake was reported and set aside. Jack, for his part, thought it faintly comic: absent-minded professors he'd heard of but absent-minded farmers were new.

A ten minute talk came next, in which Henry set out what were absolutely necessary expenses for the farm: fuel for the tractor and Land Rover and their upkeep, electricity for the milking parlour, feed for the livestock, seed for barley or other intended fodder, vet's bills, certification, any repairs on machinery, wages, upkeep of buildings, tax . . .

'You don't mention anything for the housekeeping,' Annie put in, shaking her head a little.

'That's a point I'm coming to. From now on, housekeeping must be a separate account. No more taking what's needed in occasional cheques from Emmerdale Farm Limited's account. A regular amount will be paid into an account in your name, Annie, and you'll be expected to manage within it.' He grinned. 'Rest assured, I don't expect you to have any problems.'

'But I've never done it that way!'

He took a moment before he answered, to be sure she was paying complete attention. 'You'll have to learn, Annie. I know it's different from what you're used to but it's time a proper method was brought in.' He turned to Jack. 'The farm will run on two separate bank accounts – one for day-to-day expenses and one for the big bills.'

'I don't see the need for that.'

'Take my word for it, Jack. It's best.' He hesitated. 'And

the cheque-books for both accounts stay with me.'

There was an angry pause. 'You mean I'm to have no funds to call on?'

'You'll have a petty cash float – so much each month. It's the way a business is run, lad – in a factory you don't have the manager popping off to buy a machine for bagging chemicals out of the same account that pays for the daily postage.'

Jack couldn't argue against that. He'd no idea how factories were managed. And besides, what did it matter? He didn't really care about the money. It was the independence that bothered him. 'How much is this "petty cash" going to amount to?' he asked.

'An agreed percentage of the monthly outgoings. That's fair, isn't it, Joe?'

Joe nodded. He had said almost nothing. He didn't want to antagonize Jack. But one big point had to be made. 'Am I in order to raise a point, Mr Chairman?'

'Yes?' Henry expected it to be about Demdyke. But to do Joe justice, he was thinking about Emmerdale as a whole so far.

'Mr Chairman, I'd like to know when Hathersage's is going to bring some revenue, and how it's to be paid for if it continues to be unproductive.'

Jack bristled. 'I was promised a free hand over Hathersage's.'

'That was before this downward slip became so rapid,' Henry said, cutting the outburst short. 'I've thought about Hathersage's and I've had to conclude that it's a big drain on Emmerdale's resources.'

'Nowt o' the sort!' cried Jack. 'One day you'll see—'

'Jack, we have to pay taxes on it and there's the cost of getting natural manures, and so on. Hathersage's has *got* to start earning money.'

'If you think I'm going to plough it up and scatter chemicals on it—'

'Nay, lad, not that. But you've got rid of most of the weeds and got some decent grass on it – that's so, isn't it, Joe?'

110

'Aye, not bad. Drainage needs attention, but if that were done, you could get clover off it.'

'Aye. So my suggestion is that we let Hathersage's—'

'Never!'

'Jack,' said Henry in a cold tone, 'let me finish a sentence, will you? I was going to say, we should let the pasturage.'

'Oh.' Jack fell silent.

'That's good, Henry,' Joe said. 'Now a lot of folk are turning away from dairying to beef production, there's a need for grass. And the prices are pretty fair at the moment. Besides,' he added, turning to his brother, 'you get natural fertilizer from the beef cattle. It's a mutual benefit.'

Matt spoke. His intervention was unexpected but to the point. 'It'd mean somebody else would have an eye to the fields for a year or so. It would mean you'd give more time to Emmerdale itself, Jack.' He didn't actually say that Jack's attention was often elsewhere, but the point went home.

'We-ell . . . ' It took another ten minutes' arguing, but Jack agreed.

Henry was very relieved. One of the biggest drains on their resources was being diminished. He could never really accept that it was right to farm Hathersage's on a special principle when the main farm was in need of funds, but at least it would no longer leak money away.

'Now, as to Dolly's idea of a shop. I've gone into this a bit, and there's no doubt it needs a lot of money put into it as a foundation. We'd have to construct the actual premises, and that would mean getting permission—'

'Nay, Dolly were thinking of just having folk come to the house,' Matt intervened.

'That's not on, Matt. Annie would be plagued by callers.'

'What are we going to sell, any road?' Joe asked.

'Well, the suggestion was butter, wool goods woven by Dolly, Annie's fresh eggs, perhaps geese at Christmas—'

'How much butter can Dolly make, exactly?'

'Er . . . About three or four pounds at a time,' said Matt.

They all looked at him. It was absurd. One customer might buy the entire day's produce. And in any case, how could a young mother with a new baby spare time to churn every day, on an old-fashioned butter-maker?

'My view, to put it plainly, is that the amount of output is too great for the probable returns. That's leaving aside the work and worry involved. Dealing with the public is no easy matter,' Henry said, thinking of his customers in the old days of the chemical industry.

'Dolly'll be disappointed,' muttered Matt, but sounded relieved.

'There's no reason at all why Dolly shouldn't go on with both enterprises and sell to Hotten as she's been doing already. And she might think about taking an occasional stall in Hotten Market or at agricultural fairs. No reason why not.'

Matt looked as if he could think of several, most of them to do with Dolly getting over-tired and over-anxious. But he said no more.

'Now,' said Henry, 'the biggest question of the meeting is how to acquire a substantial sum to clear off some debts and start again with a bit behind us. I have to tell you that I wouldn't feel happy without at least some capital other than the land and buildings. Any ideas?'

Joe put up his hand.

'Mr Chairman, I'd like to offer a solution to that problem. I reckon the house I'm renting from the farm is worth about twenty thousand pounds on the open market. I'd like to offer that amount for the freehold.'

He heard his mother draw in her breath, and turned to look at her.

She had understood at once. He could only want the cottage because he was planning to have Barbara move in permanently.

Chapter Nine

When Barbara returned from the conference in Lincoln, it was clear that it had been as businesslike as she intended. She seemed pleased with it. Turner, on the other hand, seemed bothered and anxious.

He had met the two directors who were to come to look at Joe's pig unit. He had got on well with Seymour, but Meadowes had proved uncommunicative. He mused over this, and came up with the ideal solution – make a social occasion of the visit, put both men entirely at their ease, and Meadowes would soon thaw.

The Spring Meeting at York was about to take place. What better than to take them there, make sure he had good tips on the horses, provide a champagne picnic, and give them a good time?

'It's just another excuse for one of his jollies,' Joe said in annoyance when he heard of it.

'He's not inviting you to be of the party, I take it!'

'No, of course not, Babs. He doesn't think I'm on his social level.' Joe frowned then laughed. 'Doesn't matter! Mum's suggested we all make a day of it at York, so I'll go with the bunch from Emmerdale. Us common folk'll have a picnic of ham sandwiches and Yorkshire brown ale!'

Annie had suggested the picnic as a way of lightening the atmosphere at Emmerdale. Jack was restless and uneasy since the board meeting with its implied criticism of his methods, and Pat had been very downcast when her pet goat was sold off. Even Matt, generally so even-tempered, had been a little put out over the complete rejection of Dolly's ideas.

The fine weather of early May had brought on a lot of work at Emmerdale. Jackie Merrick was fed up because he was still no nearer buying the motorbike he longed for to

113

whizz about the county. 'Even if I save every penny from my job at Hotten, it'll take me years to get that bike,' he mourned.

Jack smiled. 'Happen you won't have to rely only on that job. Wi' the money we get from Joe for Demdyke, we can make a lot of changes on the farm. Might mean a proper, well-paying job for you, lad.'

Annie looked up in surprise at the suggestion. In the first place she didn't want Joe to buy Demdyke. In the second, she'd imagined Jack was dead against it. Her father, who had been drowsing over last week's *Courier*, picked up the point. 'Thought you didn't like Henry's notions about modernizing?'

'We-ell . . . There's no denying there are things we could do with. I mean, if milk's going to be less of a money-earner, we've got to extend ourselves somehow.'

'Thinking of going into beef raising?'

'Dunno. I haven't really thought it through. But if Joe's really going to get twenty thousand from a building society, we could certainly use it.'

Old Sam nodded in approval. Annie thought it only wise to remind him that conditions had changed. 'You'd have to get Henry's agreement to any plans,' she reminded her son. 'Don't forget, you agreed he should control the funds from now on, lad.'

Jack's dark brows drew together. A depression set in. Knowing the signs, Pat tried to divert him by suggesting things they could do now the weather had improved – and it was then Annie suggested an outing to York Races.

Alan Turner's plans were on a somewhat grander scale, of course. But he omitted to put Barbara in the picture. She got ready all the documents needed to show the two men what was intended about expanding the pig unit, but when she tried to spread them out for their attention, Turner waved her away.

'There's time for all that later,' he said. 'Let's get in the right mood for the day, eh?' He advanced on the tray of sherry and biscuits which Barbara, at his orders, had placed ready. 'You want some of this, Ralph?'

Ralph Seymour looked at it askance. 'Got anything stronger?'

'Whisky? How about you, Meadowes?'

'I'll stick to sherry, thanks. A bit early in the day for me, actually.'

Of the two men, Barbara preferred Meadowes. He was affable, yet there was a distance between him and the others. Ralph Seymour on the other hand was full of bonhomie, but that was perhaps due to the fact that he was very keen on horse-racing, as evidenced by the copy of the *Sporting Life* he produced from his jacket pocket.

Barbara had learned she was expected to be of their party at the races. This had put a crimp in her own plans – she'd wanted to spend the time with Joe and his family in hopes of getting to know his mother better. But Turner insisted he needed her to help entertain these important men from head office.

She was therefore very prettily dressed in a soft suit of blue wool and a little hat that set off her new hairdo. Mr Seymour was very admiring. She took good care not to sit next him when they set off for York.

The racecourse was a hive of activity – programme sellers, tic-tac men, bookmakers, punters studying the race card, pretty girls out for the day, families with children in tow. The noise was great and yet it was pleasant. From time to time it died down when the public address system boomed out information, and in one of those moments Barbara, to her dismay, heard Seymour questioning Turner about her.

'Where did you find her, eh?'

'She lives in the district.'

'Lucky you! How long you had her around?'

'Only a couple of months.'

'But you've made the most of 'em, eh?'

'She's a very good secretary,' Turner said, embarrassed.

'I bet she is! Good at most things, I'd imagine!'

'Actually,' Turner said in desperation, 'she's the vicar's daughter.'

Seymour laughed. ' "She was only a vicar's daughter . . ." ' he began.

'Shhh,' urged Turner, and the other man let the joke die.

It was therefore only to be expected that Barbara put as much distance as she could between herself and Turner's party for the rest of the day. She soon fell in with the Sugdens, and by means of tips from Joe actually won some money.

She met Turner at the bookies looking fed up. 'How did you do?' she asked kindly.

'Lost a packet. How about you? No luck, I suppose, you being a total amateur.'

'Not bad,' she said, 'not bad,' and tucked the money into her bag.

Both Seymour and Meadowes had won a few pounds, so Turner had no real reason to be displeased with the day, since the whole idea had been to give the VIPs a good time. All the same, it would have been nice if he hadn't lost money himself. It would also have been nice if Barbara hadn't managed to get lost among the Sugdens for most of the events.

Back at Home Farm, Barbara valiantly tried to get the day's work going at last. She once more produced the documents she had so carefully prepared from information supplied by Joe.

But Turner waved them aside. 'Plenty of time for that when we've made ourselves comfy,' he said, dispensing drinks and gesturing towards the armchairs.

'But Alan, it's a quarter past six and I'm going out at seven.'

He stared. It hadn't occurred to him that she'd make a personal date on a day he'd told her was so important.

'I'm afraid you'll have to stick around,' he told her in a low voice.

She shook her head, but didn't argue. She didn't want a scene in front of the biggies from HQ.

Meadowes said: 'Do you do a lot of overtime here? I'd hardly have thought there was that much work.'

'No, very seldom,' she said, too fast for Turner to prevent her. He had wanted to say that his workload was so heavy he was often here burning the midnight oil.

But it was just as well he didn't for Seymour was ready with a joke. 'Too bad, old man,' he said with heavy sympathy. 'Quite a perk, staying late at the office with company like this.'

Barbara moved towards him with a little dish of peanuts and salt biscuits to go with the drink. 'Oh, thanks, little lady,' he said. She let him get his fingers into the dish then tilted it so that all the contents slipped into his lap. 'Damnation!' he said.

'So sorry,' she apologized, and moved off.

For the next twenty minutes a foursided duel was played. Seymour wanted to make a good impression on her, Alan Turner was trying to elbow her into a position where she had to stay (otherwise, he implied, she'd put him in a hole). Meadowes was putting in an occasional query, whose pointedness Turner didn't seem to notice in his eagerness to please Seymour. As for Barbara, she was sidestepping them all and wishing herself elsewhere.

'What time are we eating?' Meadowes inquired at last.

'Er . . . Any minute now. I've had it catered here, you see – firm at Harrogate does it very nicely, we'll find it all in the oven waiting to be served up.' He looked at Barbara expectantly.

'What are we having? Game, eh? Nice hot game casserole – just the job.' Seymour too was looking at Barbara.

'I'm afraid I've no idea,' Barbara said. 'I made the telephone arrangement with the caterers but I left the menu to them.'

'Well, let's see what we've got,' Turner urged, taking her by the elbow and steering her towards the door.

It opened to admit Joe Sugden. 'Oh, you're just on your way, are you?' he asked as she confronted him in the doorway. 'Come on then.'

'Joe!' exclaimed Turner, aghast.

'Who?' said Meadowes. 'Joe who?'

'Er . . . er . . . It's Joe Sugden, my assistant.'

'Come in, come in, young feller.' Meadowes studied Joe coldly. 'As I recall, the man's actual title is farm manager.'

'Er . . . Yes . . . Well, of course. But he is my assistant too.'

'Really? I'd have thought an estate manager and a secretary would get through all the work? However . . . ' He waited.

Turner had no choice but to introduce Joe. Seymour was quite uninterested, anxious only to have Barbara get to her role in the kitchen. Meadowes nodded without enthusiasm. Joe for his part was taken aback at finding them sitting around with drinks. He'd thought that by now they'd be in a huddle over his plan for modernizing the pig unit.

But if they weren't, it was no skin off his nose. He was here to collect Barbara. 'Ready?'

'Yes, just coming.'

'Barbara!' complained Turner.

'It's seven o'clock,' she said, showing him her wrist-watch. 'I did tell you I had a date at seven.' She turned sweetly to the others. 'I hope you enjoy the meal. Goodnight.'

She went out, leaving Turner flummoxed and Seymour disappointed. 'I *say*! That's not at all what I expected!'

'No . . . er . . . She . . . '

'Let's go and see if this food is ready,' said Meadowes, who by now was really hungry and, quite clearly, exasperated.

It didn't help when they found that no one had laid the table in the dining room.

'What was all that about?' Joe inquired as he drove Barbara towards their evening engagement with friends in Leeds.

'You may well ask! I think I was expected to stay and play The Hostess with the Mostest.'

'One day I'll thump that bloke,' Joe growled.

'Please don't. He's not worth it.'

'How they can let him bamboozle them with all that hospitality!'

Barbara sighed and shrugged, then changed the subject.

But Joe was still annoyed every time he thought of the scene that had met his eyes when he arrived – Turner with one hand on Barbara's elbow and a drink in the other, Seymour sprawled like a lord in an armchair, Meadowes standing looking down his nose.

And to make things worse, when Joe went to inspect the pig unit next day, he found the head pigman in a state bordering on tears. 'Joe, I don't know how to tell you this! We lost twelve piglets during the night!'

'You what? Lost 'em? How d'you mean?' Joe was horrified. Please God, not some awful infection to run through the whole unit!

'Some fool left the door of the farrowing house open!'

It was never established how it happened. But when Joe heard that after dinner Turner had taken his guests to inspect the unit, he had no doubt that one of them was responsible for the carelessness.

He drove back far too fast and stormed into the Home Farm office. 'You and your nobs from Headquarters!' he cried. 'D'you know what you've done?'

Turner rose from his desk. 'I'll have a quieter tone, thank you,' he said. 'What's the matter with you?'

'Twelve piglets dead, and Tim fighting to save another three! The temperature in the farrowing house went down eleven degrees during the night!'

'It did?' Turner was still a long way from understanding the situation. 'A fault in the thermostat system?'

'A fault in the human supervision system—'

'Oh, then, I hope you've given Tim Huller a piece of your mind.'

'It's nowt to do with Tim! Some idiot walked out and left the door open behind him!'

'What?' Turner said, losing colour a little.

'You and your posh friends from Lincoln! You haven't

got the sense of a little maid in a milkshop! Do you know what you've done? You've—'

'I suppose it's wiped out the profits of two or three weeks of—'

'The profits! Aye! But not only that! It's wiped out the lives of twelve animals and maybe more – we're *responsible* for them—'

'Oh, come on now, Joe. Don't let's get emotional over pigs!'

'I've a right to be emotional! I've a right to raise the roof! What's the use of all the work of the last six months, upgrading the unit and getting better breeding stock, if all that happens is you let them die of cold?'

'Me?' Turner said. 'I didn't leave any doors open behind me.'

'Who, then? The red-faced one – Seymour? Or him with the mouth like a rat-trap? I warn you, Turner, I'm not going to let this go without somebody getting a roasting!'

'Indeed?' said the estate manager, smiling with superiority. 'What are you going to do? Drive to Lincoln and have it out with them?'

'I want a report made out.'

'Don't be naive. I'm writing no report that blames a director!'

'You're not? So how are you going to account for the loss? Twelve pedigree piglets – fifteen, happen.'

'I'll write it off as equipment failure.'

'You'll do nothing of the sort! I checked that equipment myself, inch by inch, when it was installed. And I've kept a close eye on it since. I'm not taking the blame for this.'

'What are you going to do, then?' Turner challenged, looking smug. 'Any report on this will have to be okayed by me. You can take it for granted, my dear chap, that I'm not blighting my career by blaming either Seymour or Meadowes.'

Joe stared at him. 'You mean you're going to tell blatant lies?'

Turner shrugged, went back to his desk, and sat down. 'I

think we've dealt with all that, Joe. I'm sure you've got work to do.'

Joe leaned over and laid a hand on the papers Turner was about to pick up. It was a big hand, and as it came down Turner flinched – for a moment he'd thought it was going to hit him.

'This isn't the end of it, Turner,' Joe said. Then he straightened, wheeled about, and stalked out.

Chapter Ten

When he thought things over, Alan Turner was alarmed at the determination he'd seen in Joe's face. Perhaps he'd been a little too curt with him. He set himself to make amends by being absolutely charming for the rest of the week.

Joe's intention to do something about the negligence over the pig unit didn't lessen. He set about writing a paper which, he told himself, he'd submit to HQ over Turner's head. But nevertheless, it was so much like telling tales that he couldn't somehow finish the report.

It was better to come out in the open with his complaints. He sought out Turner on the following Saturday. 'Alan, it's time you and I had a heart-to-heart.'

'About what? If it's the silage, the spare parts are on their way.'

'It's not that, Alan. I want to tell you, straight out and honest, that I don't like the way the estate is run.'

Turner's mouth fell open. After a speechless moment he gasped: 'Have you lost your mind?'

'What, because I think you make a mess of things? Or because I dare to tell you so?'

It was the latter, of course. And Turner coloured up at the words. 'Let me tell you, Joe, I've a lot of experience—'

'Of wriggling out of corners you get yourself into by your lack of grip. I know, I've watched you.' Joe sighed deeply. 'I'm not enjoying this, Alan. But the way you were prepared to tell lies over the loss of those piglets really sickened me. And the way you—'

'What?'

'The way you presented Babs to those chaps from Headquarters. It was easy to see they thought she was there for a kiss and a cuddle.'

'Now look here, Joe!'

'Don't ruffle up your feathers and play indignant. You know as well as I do that that feller who smelt of whisky thought Babs was going to let him hold her hand, to say the least of it. And you never actually showed them any of those figures about the pig unit.'

'I did!'

'No you didn't. They were still in their folders untouched the next morning.'

'And how can you possibly know that?'

'Babs told me.'

'So . . . She tells tales behind my back, does she?'

'She's employed by NY Estates to help you run the place. She was totally within her rights to let me know you hadn't presented those figures. Now, look here, Alan, don't try to get out of it by working up a grudge against Barbara. You know you let the whole thing get out of hand – God knows how much liquor you swallowed – but by the time the evening ended I should think none of you were capable of even seeing a row of figures, let alone understanding 'em.'

'That's quite enough, Sugden! I think you should remember who you are! You're nothing but a junior manager!'

'I know who I am. Question is, do you know who you are? Are you a huntin', shootin', and fishin' squire, a wily businessman, or a farming expert? I'm sick and tired of never knowing which hat you're wearing. Not that any of them fit you all that well.'

'You dare to—'

'Aw, dry up! You *know* you're at a loss half the time. I daresay it's that very fact that makes you play the little Napoleon.'

'Let me tell you, Sugden, you've gone far too far this time! I've put up with your ignorance and insubordination, heaven knows,' cried Turner, 'but this is too much! After the way I've shielded you—'

'You've shielded me? What a fairy tale!'

'What about that time you mixed up the weedkiller and the insect spray?'

'I didn't do that and you know it – it was your white-headed boy from Lincolnshire. And so were most of the other things you're going to bring up – things you messed up first and then put on to me. It took me a long time to get your number, Alan, but I've finally—'

'You've finally shown yourself as what you are – disloyal, deceitful—'

'Oh aye? Is that why you've been buttering me up all week – because you think I'm a rat?'

'We won't discuss my opinion of you. Let me just say that NY Estates can get on very well without you, Sugden.'

'Right you are,' Joe said. 'If I'm such a total loss and you want to get rid of me, that makes it even – because I want to go. I'm ready to let you have my resignation any time.'

Alan Turner went quite white. It was almost like a physical blow. Lose Joe Sugden?

Who would handle the men if he went? Who understood their Yorkshire sense of humour, their quiet stubbornness against uppity behaviour? Who would manage the pedigree records? Who would understand the ins and outs of the expanded pig unit? Who knew the land and the local weather conditions, the neighbouring farmers, the traditions and habits of centuries?

Who else but Joe Sugden?

'Now, wait a minute . . . don't let bad temper force you into a step—'

'It's not bad temper and I'm not being forced into it. It's fed-upness, and I've thought it over. I don't enjoy my work any more, Turner. Everything's going sour – and it's not because of the place, it's because of the conditions. I'm sick of carrying the can for your mistakes. I'm sick of being patronized. And I'm sick of the sort of dishonesty that surrounds everything.'

'Dishonesty? I'm not dishonest, Joe! You misunderstand – the truth isn't always advisable in business—'

'That's just the attitude I'm complaining of. Nobody

expects us to be angels, but for heaven's sake, let's at least not tell downright lies! But beyond that there's the feeling that you're only furthering your own career – that you don't really care about the estate or the people who get their living through it. I'm part of this dale, Turner. And unless things change around here, I can't stay to see it being manipulated to put you in a cushy job in Lincoln.'

'Don't take any decisions based on emotion, Joe,' pleaded Turner, thoroughly scared. 'There's no sentiment in business, you know. And you've a career here that you shouldn't throw away.'

'A career! Huh!'

'Yes you have, yes you have! I've already recommended you to HQ for promotion.'

This was a total untruth and both men knew it. However, there was this much value in it – Turner might in the near future put something favourable in the annual report he had to do on the estate staff.

Joe said: 'Promotion would be nice. But what I want for the moment is some respect for my position here. I'm sick of being treated like a pawn in your chess game.'

'It's not like that, Joe, I assure you – it never was. But if that's how you saw it, I'm sorry. I can tell you, from now on I'll take especial care.'

'Aye,' Joe said in a hard tone, 'you better had, Alan. For I can tell you, as far as I'm concerned, you've had as much rope as I'm ready to give you. Next time there's a crisis, I might just let you go hang.'

When he looked back on it afterwards, Turner couldn't believe he'd really been frightened. Joe Sugden would never leave his job. What would he do? He couldn't go back to farming at Emmerdale – his brother Jack would be miffed at having him breathing down his neck. And no matter how honest and high-minded you were, jobs as farm managers were hard to come by.

All the same, better safe than sorry. He'd better not think of Sugden as an underling any more – the man could be dangerous.

125

He had another shock coming to him. Late that Saturday, there was a call from head office. It was Arnold Meadowes. 'Turner? I thought I'd let you know – I'll be back at Home Farm on Monday.'

'Really?' cried Turner. 'Er . . . any particular reason?'

'The board want a few things investigated.'

'Investigated?' It was a whisper of near-despair.

'I'll be staying at the Feathers in Connelton. No need to lay on catering for me,' Meadowes said, with what sounded like irony. 'But I'd like the estate books ready to hand, and the reports on forward budgeting.'

'Yes. Yes, of course. Anything else?'

'I want the staff records.' There was a tiny pause. 'Yours included.'

'Yes, Mr Meadowes,' Turner said faintly.

Joe had already left for Demdyke. Turner's first instinct was to drive there and demand that he help man the defences. But first he had a stiff whisky to bolster his morale, and then he thought better of it. Joe was so confoundedly *honest* – it was no use expecting him to take part in a cover-up. And the problem was, Turner didn't know which part of his management to shroud in secrecy – he really had no idea what Mr Meadowes intended to do.

Joe would have been relatively unworried had he known of Meadowes' impending visit. He was at that moment trying to persuade Barbara to think seriously about re-marriage.

'But, Joe, Brian and I have never even talked about divorce!'

'But that's how it's going to end, isn't it? I mean, you aren't thinking of ever going back to him.'

'Of course not.' Barbara and Joe both knew that a reconciliation was ruled out by the seriousness of the relationship that had grown up between them. 'But it's one thing to walk out on your marriage. It's quite another going to court and having it officially ended.'

'Still, you've got to start thinking about the future, haven't you? The time's got to come when—'

'Why is everybody in such a hurry to push me into

126

decisions?' she cried in a sort of panicky despair. 'I don't know what I want to do, Joe. I haven't thought further than just having my life to myself for a bit.'

If Joe had been wise, he would have left it there. They were walking home together towards the vicarage, and the privacy of the Beckindale lanes in the dusk had prompted him to start on this important subject.

He wanted to stake a claim on her, so that when she came to think about her future she would include him in it. 'All I was thinking was, about Demdyke . . . '

'What about Demdyke?'

'I know it's not much of a place, but we could make it a lot nicer.'

'We?'

'Well, of course you must know, Babs. I want us to—'

She shook her head vehemently. 'It's not the time to start talking about what you want for "us" – I've still not separated myself from Brian.'

'But you're going to, aren't you? I mean, look here, love – let's have some idea where we stand, eh?'

'Well . . . Yes . . . I've decided to start divorce proceedings. But I haven't done anything about it so far.'

'But you will?'

'Ye-es,' she said. She couldn't yet picture herself going to a lawyer and saying, 'Write to my husband and tell him it's all over.' But the time would come, she supposed.

'Well, then,' urged Joe.

'Let's leave it till then, if you don't mind.'

'But, Babs, there's a lot to be thought of—'

'Leave it, I said!' They were at the corner of Vicarage Lane. She walked smartly away from him. 'Bye for now, Joe.'

Thus dismissed, he stood uncertain, watching her reach the gate of the vicarage and go in. She was lost to view among the shrubbery that masked the old house unless you were actually at the gate.

He cursed himself. Why couldn't he let well alone?

He didn't fancy the solitude of Demdyke for an evening

meal. He turned his steps back to where he'd left the Land Rover and drove to Emmerdale. There his mother welcomed him as usual: the coolness between them since the christening party seemed to have died away.

Annie Sugden had wrestled with herself over her son's actions. She wanted to prevent him from doing wrong, yet her sense of his importance told her she ought not to interfere. All the same, she wanted to know whether this was just some casual interlude or whether it meant something serious to him. When the meal was over and there had been some family chat, she accompanied him out to his transport.

'You seem a bit down?' she remarked.

He shrugged.

'Things going all right at NY?'

'You must be joking. I've got it in mind to chuck the whole thing.'

'Joe!'

'I mean it. I've had Alan Turner up to here!' He put his hand up to his throat. 'You've no idea what it's like, Ma. He's just never straight about anything.'

'But what would you do, Joe? It's a very good job to throw away.'

He sighed. 'That's the problem, isn't it? Jobs like that don't grow on trees.'

'You could always come back to Emmerdale.'

'Nay, Ma . . . I wouldn't fit in here any more.'

'Joe, don't talk like that! There's always a place here for you!'

But even as she said it, she wondered if it was true. In the first place, Joe had changed. He was no longer the open, eager, enthusiastic young man who had managed the small farm. He had achieved a little sophistication, enough to seem to belong to a larger world than Emmerdale.

And then there was her elder son . . . She could imagine the disagreements that would follow if Joe wanted to import some of the ideas he'd learned at NY Estates. Joe was easygoing, certainly – but he knew his own mind and wouldn't take kindly to being quashed by an amateur like Jack. And the fact was that Jack was the manager of Emmerdale now. He was the eldest, the inheritor – everyone acknowledged that. In the end it was what he said that counted.

'We'd be a bit crowded, wouldn't we, Ma?' Joe pointed out. 'A lot to earn a livelihood for – there's how many of us – eight if you count Baby Sam. With me, that'd be nine. And what if I wanted to get married?'

She hesitated. 'Do you think you will get married again, Joe?'

If only he knew! He said, with deep uncertainty, 'It don't depend on me. It's what *she* feels that matters.'

They both knew he was talking about Barbara. 'Have you talked about it to her?'

'She shies off . . . It's understandable. But you see, Ma, that's one of the reasons why I hang on at NY, instead of walking out. I've got to have a job and some prospects to offer her, haven't I?'

Annie tried to imagine Barbara Peters fitting in at Emmerdale as a sort of third house-help after herself and Pat – and quite failed to picture it. If she had to be honest, she would have said that Barbara simply wouldn't fit in at Emmerdale. When – if – she and Joe married, they would have to have a place of their own.

Hence Joe's wish to buy Demdyke, of course.

'You'd best take it carefully, lad,' she advised. Already she was thinking of Joe married to Barbara, settled in Beckindale in a modernized version of Demdyke. Everything would be better, once they were a married couple. Better for herself and Barbara's father, but most of all better for the young folk, for it was easy to see Joe was genuinely in love.

The following Monday, Arnold Meadowes arrived. Joe had by now learned of his impending visit. It amazed him to see how much it perturbed Turner.

'What're you in such a tizz about?' he asked. 'We do

129

our jobs – that's all he can ask.'

'You just don't understand! There's something up, or he wouldn't be here.'

Joe refused to let it worry him. He would stand or fall by what he had done at NY Estates.

Meadowes arrived prompt at nine, commandeered the old sitting room of Home Farm as an office, and settled in there with the invoices and accounts. Turner at first kept putting his head round the door to offer coffee, information, a sandwich . . . But in the end he got the message – Mr Meadowes wished to be left alone.

'I can't think why you're so bothered,' Joe said, with hidden irony. 'You've nothing to be worried about, have you, Alan?'

'If Meadowes wants us to be worried, he'll find something,' Turner said, his broad face sagging with unhappiness.

At lunchtime the investigator announced he'd go for a walk to stretch his legs. 'What about a meal, Mr Meadowes?' inquired Turner. 'I've provisionally booked a table—'

'Don't bother about that. I'll get a snack somewhere, don't you worry.'

And with that Alan Turner had to be satisfied.

Arnold Meadowes went for a stroll around NY's domain. Either by design or accident, his steps took him to the pig unit. There he found Tim Huller, the head pigman, sitting in his little office with a substantial sandwich and a flask of tea. 'Mind if I come in?'

Tim half-rose. He looked distinctly unwelcoming. 'I were just having me snap,' he said.

'That's all right, you just go ahead.'

It's well-nigh impossible to eat heartily when someone else is looking on. Tim knew he ought to offer at least a cup of his tea, but he was hanged if he was going to be polite to this idiot who'd lost him twelve piglets.

Meadowes began a conversation about the pig-house. All he got was monosyllables. Finally he said in some

130

surprise: 'Have you got some objection to my being here, Huller?'

'Last time you were here,' Tim burst out, pushing away his sandwich with a big, angry hand, 'you caused a tragedy!'

'Eh?' Meadowes was truly taken aback.

'Twelve little bodies! An' they were lively and happy when I went off duty that evening!'

'What?' cried Meadowes. 'What're you on about, man?'

'You left the door of the farrowing house open! The temperature went down so low that twelve piglets died! And you call yourself a manager!'

'Twelve piglets?'

'Aye, and it was only 'cos Joe and I worked all day and the next night on 'em that we didn't lose three more!'

Nowhere in the account books that Meadowes had just examined was there any mention about the loss of twelve valuable piglets. Nor was it in the record-book, the commonplace book kept of day-to-day affairs.

'I assure you, Huller,' said Meadowes, '*I* didn't leave the door open. I left the others here while I went back to the office to look for the paper Joe Sugden had done about extending the unit . . . ' Yes, and couldn't find it because Alan Turner had somehow covered it with other documents during the evening.

While he was still looking for it Seymour and Turner came back, roaring with laughter at some drunken joke. Fed up with both of them, Meadowes had at last managed to persuade Seymour it was time to go, had driven him back to the Feathers and poured him into bed. He himself had sat thinking for half an hour before he retired.

It was due to those thoughts that he'd done a report which had asked for the investigation he was now pursuing.

'I'm sorry about the piglets,' he said. 'You took it to heart, clearly.'

'Aye,' Huller said, grudgingly softening his manner. 'An' so did Joe – I never saw him so angry.' He hesitated. 'Have a cup of my tea,' he offered. 'It's a bit strong for most tastes but you can water it down wi' water from the heater.'

By and by, Meadowes wended his way to the village. There he came on Joe Sugden coming out of the shop with a newspaper. 'Hello, there. Keeping up with the great world?' he asked, nodding at it.

Joe shrugged. To tell the truth, he'd bought it for the job columns. 'Getting all the information you need?' he countered.

'I've just been talking to your head pigman. Very interesting.'

He saw Joe stiffen, and waited for the outburst of accusation that ought to follow. But Joe drew a deep breath and said: 'Oh aye?'

'I suppose Turner was very upset about the loss of the piglets,' prompted Meadowes.

'I think so.'

'What's your view on it?'

Joe chose not to reply directly. 'What did Alan's report say?'

Well, that was a good try, thought Meadowes. But he'd fallen into the trap all the same, for it showed he thought there would be a report on the loss – and in fact there was none.

Which only proved that Turner was single-handedly covering up the inefficiency that surfaced from time to time in the management of NY's Beckindale properties.

'I've never yet seen that paper you wrote about expanding the pig unit. In fact, it seems to have got lost. Do you happen to have a copy yourself?'

Joe shook his head. 'Only my rough notes.'

'Could I see those?'

'Oh, but surely there must be a typed copy in the office?'

'Just let me see your notes,' ordered Meadowes. That way, he didn't have to let Turner know he was looking into the matter. It was quite clear that Turner didn't want Joe's report to be seen as it stood, and this must be for reasons of his own. Perhaps it was because it was a very bad report and would make NY management think them a bunch of fools.

On the other hand, perhaps it was a very good report. In

which case, it was being repressed because Turner didn't want Joe to get the credit.

Meadowes had a long memory. There had been an excellent paper Joe had written after attending a special course in Scotland about beef production. Because of that, NY Estates was slowly moving from milk to the raising of lean beef. Perhaps Joe's new report would encourage them to go profitably into pork production.

Whatever the result, Meadowes wanted to see that paper.

The one he got was a typed copy that Barbara had kept for her own records and which she gladly supplied when Joe confided his problem. She smiled as she handed it over. 'If Meadowes mentions this to Alan, it'll give him a shock. He's locked all the other copies in the safe in the stores-room.'

'You what?' gasped Joe.

'Oh, Joe, you're so honest it hurts! Of *course* Alan doesn't want Meadowes to see that report – that's why he's got rid of all the copies.'

'But those two chaps came on purpose to look at the idea, Barbara—'

'Yes, and Alan managed to turn their attention to a day at the races. He hoped nothing more would be heard of it.'

'But that's daft! Anything that increases NY's profits here in Beckindale is good for him.'

'Not if he has to give you the credit. That idea would have re-surfaced next year, and I'll give you three guesses whose name would be attached to it then.'

Joe shook his head. He couldn't actually believe anyone would be so devious.

For the next few days Arnold Meadowes came and went like a great looming thundercloud. He resisted all Turner's attempts to organize his work. He turned up where he wasn't expected, and he seldom smiled. In fact, he seemed to get grimmer and grimmer as the week approached its end.

'I've a feeling I'm going to get the sack,' Joe told his mother when he rang her to let her know how things were going.

'Oh, Joe, you've got the wrong impression—'

'Nay, Ma, he's right fed up with what he's seen, you can tell that.'

'But the land is well-farmed.'

'Oh aye, there's nowt wrong wi' the land. But from little things he's let drop, you can tell he don't think too much of the management.'

'But surely that's Mr Turner's job, not yours?'

'Oh, it's down to me as well, Ma. I'm not kidding myself. He thinks nowt of either of us, I reckon.'

Annie couldn't help but be worried by what he was saying. But she refused to let her anxiety show. 'Don't you take it to heart, lad. Even if worst comes to worst, there's other places you can go.'

But as she put down the receiver she was only too well aware that Emmerdale wasn't likely to be one of them. She'd discussed this possibility with Henry Wilks already, and his reaction had not been good.

'There's not enough income from Emmerdale land to make a viable job for Joe,' he had said. 'You only have to look at the figures . . . '

'Oh, Henry, don't talk to me about figures! I'm talking about my son's career – there must be some way we can help him if things go wrong at NY.'

Henry sighed. She was the best of women, and yet she was like all the rest – she didn't want to look facts in the face when her heart told her not to.

'I'll think on it, love,' he said. But he didn't sound optimistic.

Barbara, who saw the situation from a different standpoint, had her own reasons for being worried. Joe wouldn't speak out against Turner to Meadowes. It wasn't in his nature. That being so, Turner would somehow change any faults so as to make them seem due to Joe's actions. And the trouble was that though she knew quite a lot of what had gone on recently, she didn't have information about past mistakes, those that had happened before she arrived on the scene.

And all of those, she was sure, had somehow been written off either as unavoidable freaks of nature or Joe's inexperience.

When she was asked for day-to-day information by Arnold Meadowes, she gave it accurately. She didn't accentuate Alan Turner's inefficiency, neither did she speak in favour of Joe. Yet she saw that Meadowes caught inflections, echoes of unspoken words.

'You happy in your job here?' he asked suddenly one day when she was searching the files for something Pat Sugden had hidden during her term of office.

She paused. 'Happy enough.'

'That's not exactly enthusiastic. Is it to do with working conditions?'

She took a moment, wishing to be entirely honest. 'The job's all right. A bit low-grade compared with what I'm used to, but beggars can't be choosers.'

'Beggars? Oh, come – a girl like you?'

'There are personal difficulties.'

'Here at the office?'

'Oh, not particularly. No, not that. It's a private matter. So for the moment I have to stick with this job because it happens to be the only one going around here.'

'I see. Well, how could we upgrade the work here so that you'd get job satisfaction?'

'Oh,' she said, shaking her head, 'I don't think that's possible. It's a small office for a small part of a large concern. There really isn't anything here to stretch me. I'm not complaining,' she added quickly. 'I knew it was small-scale when I took it on.'

'How about the personal side?' he continued, reaching the point where she knew he'd been aiming all along. 'Get on well with everyone?'

'Quite well, thank you.'

'Boss considerate and all that?'

She looked at him with her expressive grey glance. 'In my experience, Mr Meadowes, secretaries can't expect too much consideration from their bosses.'

'Do you feel Mr Turner has consideration for you?'

'Mr Meadowes, you've been here five days now. Surely you've drawn some conclusions.'

'I was also here a week ago for a short visit. Does that kind of thing often happen here?'

'What kind of thing?'

'Are you often expected to act as hostess?'

'Mr Turner's wife doesn't live at the farm. It's only natural that I'm called on to act as stand-in hostess now and again.' She paused. 'A lot depends on the guests, of course.'

'Ye-es . . . ' He gave his grim smile. 'What kind of guests does Mr Turner have, as a rule?'

'That must have shown up in the account for entertaining expenses. He has a lot of business with chain-store butchers and big feed-merchants, and of course the shooting here is very useful in offering a good atmosphere in which to discuss business.'

'I'd have thought pointing a gun at a bird was just the wrong moment to discuss business.'

'You know what I mean – the atmosphere afterwards.'

'And you stay around then?'

She shook her head vehemently. 'Not at all. Your friend Mr Seymour was a little unusual, if that's what you're asking, Mr Meadowes.'

'I quite agree. Ralph Seymour is regarded as a "character" by his colleagues. Well, Mrs Peters, this has been a very useful chat. Thank you.' He turned as if to go, then came back. 'What do you think of the farm manager?' he asked as if in afterthought.

'Joe?'

'Yes. What do you think of him – as farm manager, I mean.'

'He's a friend of mine. You wouldn't expect me to be critical.'

Meadowes cocked his eyebrow. 'I notice you didn't say that about your employer.'

She made no reply.

'What do you think of Sugden?' he insisted.

'If you must know, I think he's wasted here!' she burst out. 'He has to carry out instructions from a man who knows less than he does. You must have seen for yourself that Joe's work on the estate is first-rate – and the men like him.' She stopped abruptly. She'd been about to say, 'Which is more than you can say for Alan.'

'Would you say that Joe Sugden is capable of bigger things?'

'Certainly.'

'Thank you. I value your opinion.'

He went back to his little makeshift office. Barbara wondered if she had spoken wisely, but couldn't believe it would harm Joe to tell the truth – which was that if one of those two men should be in charge of NY interests in Beckindale, it ought to be Joe.

Later that afternoon Meadowes let it be known he wished the estate and farm managers to be available in the Home Farm office. He took up the position where Turner usually sat, behind the desk. He had a sheaf of papers in front of him, in apple pie order.

The two men sat uneasily on chairs across from him – like applicants for a job. And in a sense that's what they were. They both knew that their careers were on the line.

'You'll understand that in a week's study it's impossible to sort out all the problems of NY's holdings in Beckindale. Of course I did some paperwork at Head Office before I came here so I had background. All the same . . . ' He eyed them above the paper he was holding, 'once on the ground here, I was surprised to see the overmanning really did exist.'

'Oh, but Mr Meadowes—'

'You're going to say you inherited that, Turner, and I accept that. But you've been here a considerable time now. You could have remedied it. It would have been better to lay off some of these men with redundancy payments than keep them on.'

'I didn't want NY to get a name for—'

'The rationalization of the farms' production has been fair. I must say the pig unit has been a success – insofar as current market difficulties allow. There have been one or two strange hiccups—' He paused, as if waiting for an interruption from Joe, but when none came he went on. 'Well, the mistakes can't be laid at your door, Sugden. I've gathered the impression that you know what you're about.'

'Thank you,' Joe muttered.

For his part, Turner shifted in his chair and looked as if he wished he were elsewhere.

'I feel you could easily assume much greater responsibility than you have had here, Joe. You're probably aware, NY have plenty of opportunities for their young hopefuls . . .'

He glanced at his notes. 'As you'd expect, there are to be some changes. Things are happening at Head Office these days and it's only right that there should be matching changes in our farms.'

'Of course, Mr Meadowes,' said Turner hopefully.

'Very well. In the first place, discretion hitherto exercised by estate managers will cease. Our computer link-up from Lincoln will make most decisions by estate managers unnecessary – a computer terminal here will enable you to feed in any queries and the answer will be supplied within minutes, taking in the larger view.'

Joe heard Alan Turner give a long, weary sigh. He couldn't help feeling sorry for the man. His job was being reduced so that he would be nothing but a puppet.

'All administrative facilities – buying, marketing, crop and livestock decisions – are to be centralized. A complete picture of the company's affairs will be available from the computer terminal at the touch of a key. Paperwork will be greatly reduced.'

Meadowes looked directly at Turner. 'This means that the status of the estate managers will be diminished, as will the workload. In that case, one of the first casualties will be your secretary, Turner. She will hardly be required in the new format of work. However, if she understands how to handle a computer you could perhaps offer her two or three days a week – certainly at first, when you have to learn how to come to terms with it yourself.'

'I can learn how to work with a computer,' Turner said, almost in a tone of pleading.

'I should hope so,' Meadowes said without bending in the least. 'Modern office techniques make that necessary. However, since your office work will be greatly reduced, I expect you to take on the role of farm manager as well.'

Joe's heart sank. It was one thing to think about chucking up the job. It was another to be given the push.

'Then that means that Joe—'

'I have plans for Joe,' Meadowes said. 'In any case, it's not the policy of the company to make its managerial staff redundant – we can usually deploy them usefully. It means, nevertheless, that you will have to move from Beckindale.'

'Where to?' Joe asked.

Meadowes hunched his shoulders and looked thoughtful. 'I haven't decided that for the moment. I want you to gain experience in some other setting so that you can move on to greater responsibility. Although you have done well here, this is home ground. You need to be stretched, in my opinion.'

'I see.'

'That's the situation. Both of you have a new challenge to face. If it doesn't suit either of you, you are of course at liberty to sever your relationship with the company.'

Joe and Turner looked at each other.

'I don't expect an immediate reply. I realize that this new situation comes as something of a surprise. But I want you to understand that the changes I have in mind are unavoidable so if you can't accept them, you had better think of a career with some other organization.' He paused, gathering up his papers. 'I should think you'll know your minds by next Friday. I hope to hear from you by then, one way or the other. That's all, gentlemen. Good evening.'

Chapter Eleven

Henry Wilks was looking thoughtful. 'The way I see it, Joe,' he said, 'this puts paid to your idea of buying Demdyke from Emmerdale Farm Limited.'

'Oh?' said Annie in surprise. 'Why?'

'Well, Ma, I'm in a cleft stick,' Joe explained. 'If I stay with NY Estates and get moved elsewhere, I don't need Demdyke. If I decide against NY Estates so as to stay in Beckindale, I don't have a job and can't get a mortgage – so I can't buy Demdyke.'

Annie looked stricken for a moment. Then she stiffened. 'We'll think of summat,' she said.

But what? Henry wondered. The proposition put to Joe by Mr Meadowes had certainly set the cat among the pigeons for the folk at Emmerdale. In a way, it was a challenge for Jack as well as for Joe. For the obvious solution was for Jack to offer his younger brother a job at Emmerdale. That wouldn't be easy, but if he would come to Henry and ask for advice on how to achieve it, Henry thought he saw how it could be done.

Henry, Joe and Annie were having an informal meeting in the back room at the Woolpack, Amos having gone out on purpose to leave them free. Amos had huffed and puffed a little about 'vacating his premises', but when told sternly by Henry that Joe's future was at stake, he'd suddenly decided he could go to interview a prize-winner at the recent darts match, on behalf of the *Hotten Courier*.

It was Joe who voiced Henry's thoughts. 'If summat's going to be "thought of", it's got to have Jack's approval,' he said. 'He's t'boss at Emmerdale now.' He rose. 'Time I was getting home,' he said. 'I haven't told Babs the news yet.'

Annie sighed inwardly at the implication in that remark –

140

that Barbara would be there in his home waiting for him.

And indeed she was. 'Bad news, was it?' she asked as he came in.

'Could have been worse, but not much,' he grunted. 'At least I didn't get the order of the boot.'

'What in fact did you get?' She was a little surprised at his air of dismay. She'd thought a promotion was in the air.

'I've got a week to make up my mind whether I'll work elsewhere for 'em. If I refuse the new job offer, I'm redundant.'

'Oh, Joe!'

'It's a clever piece of thinking. If I refuse the new job and take redundancy, I don't get a penny. That's the rules.'

'Yes, I know . . . Joe, what sort of job are they offering?'

'Oh, it's made to sound like some sort of promotion. I'm supposed to move on somewhere to learn more, to make me fit for bigger things—'

'But that's good, Joe.'

'It's a load of old nonsense! Meadowes took a look at the pair of us, Turner and me, and decided to get shot of one of us. The one they're keeping had to be capable of playing second fiddle to a computer so they picked on Turner, Oh!' he said stricken by recollection. 'The news for you ain't too good either, love.'

'Me? Oh, well . . . ' Her shrug said that she never thought much of the job anyhow.

'In view of a computer link-up with Head Office, there won't be as much work for a secretary, so Turner's to offer you about three days a week. If you teach him to handle the computer, which is part of the deal, I think you can put yourself out of a job even faster.'

She considered it. Then she rose from the armchair where she'd been curled. 'I'll make us some coffee, shall I? Or would you prefer something stronger?'

'Coffee'd be fine.' He came after her to the kitchen, watched her fill the kettle and get mugs down from the hooks. 'What gets my goat is that it's so unfair! Turner's the one that's caused all the problems, and he's the one that's left sitting pretty.'

'It's hardly sitting pretty, darling. As far as I can gather from what you say, he's been turned into a glorified office boy.'

'But with no reduction in pay, I gather. And he's left in a cushy spot, with his accommodation still assured.'

'Whereas you?' she prompted.

'I've been pushed down a step.'

'Oh, I don't think it's exactly a demotion, Joe.'

'You can't be more demoted than told you have to move on elsewhere or take the sack!'

'You haven't been sacked!' And before he could interrupt she swept on: 'You've no idea what kind of job they have in mind for you. There are a lot of plum positions in NY, I bet.'

'How can it be a plum position if it's all gonna be done by computers wherever you go, Babs?'

The kettle boiled, staving off an answer for a moment. She poured hot water on the coffee granules. As she offered him the steaming mug she said: 'Meadowes gave no hint of what he's got in mind for you?'

'Not him! He's made it like a sort of obstacle course – he's not going to say what sort of job it is until I say whether I'm taking it.'

Barbara sat down at the kitchen table, sipping her coffee before replying. 'It's a funny way of handling personnel,' she said. 'I don't think it's even legal to expect staff to accept a pig in a poke like that.'

'What am I supposed to do? Challenge Meadowes and get chucked out on my ear straight away?'

'No . . . Perhaps not. In a way, Joe . . . it's a kind of character test, I think.'

'You what?'

'He wants to know if you have courage enough to take a step that he's offering.'

'Walk the plank blindfold, you mean.'

142

'Well, he's standing by. If you just balk at it, he'll let you stand or fall on your own. But if you trust him . . . it may do you a lot of good.'

'Humph,' said Joe, totally unconvinced.

There was a silence while they considered the new future that Meadowes had opened before them. Then Joe set down his coffee-mug, stretching out his hand along the table to Barbara.

'If I took a job away from here, would you come with me?'

She coloured a little. 'I can't answer that, Joe.'

'But would you think about it?'

'Ye-es . . . Yes, I'd think about it.'

And with that he had to be content.

Henry Wilks used next day, Saturday, following up a rumour he'd heard. A farmer called Stanley Wetherall was said to be selling up, due to his retirement and the fact that he had no son interested in keeping on the farm.

The tale proved to be true. Wetherall, a friendly, voluble character, smiled when he saw Henry climb out of his car in the farmyard. 'Hey-up! News gets round!'

'Well, if you start putting your equipment on the market, Stan, folk are bound to draw conclusions.'

'Aye . . . Well, I take it you're interested in some of the stuff? The disc harrow's almost new, and there's a half-track—'

'Nay, lad, it's not about the equipment. It's the farm.'

'You're never going to say you want to buy the farm?'

'Why not, Stan?'

'That Jack Sugden of yours couldn't manage another stretch of land in addition to what he's got! He's not doing too well, I hear—'

'How d'you hear that?'

'Oh, he was seen going into the bank looking anxious and coming out looking flummoxed. Nay, Henry, where would you get cash to buy Rowan Farm?'

'We'd get it,' Henry said.

'Chuck more of your own money down t'drain, eh? I'd have thought you'd done enough of that already, what with Hathersage's . . . ' Wetherall smiled. 'Mind you, that land'll end up the most fertile stretch in t'Dales. But at what a price, eh?'

'Stan, I didn't come here for a lecture on farming economics. Are you selling the farm, yes or no?'

'Well . . . aye, I am.'

'Now that that's established, let's go indoors out of this drizzle and talk about money.'

'Nowt like inviting yourself in,' Wetherall said, laughing at Henry's directness. 'Right, lad, let's see what kind of money you're willing to put up.'

The interview – argument, rather – was long and not very productive as far as Henry was concerned. Wetherall wanted to sell the land to a farmer. He didn't want to see his farm get lost in NY Estates property. But he wasn't going to let it go for nothing. He had his old age to think of and prices were high.

The following day, Sunday, Henry called at Emmerdale when he thought Annie might be alone after lunch. The weather had improved so Jack had taken Pat out for a drive. Jackie was off helping a friend dismantle an old motorbike for spare parts, Sam was in his vegetable garden.

'Annie, I think I've solved our problem,' he said.

'About Joe?'

He nodded. 'I think we can make a job for Joe at Emmerdale by buying Stan Wetherall's land and adding it to Emmerdale Farm Limited.'

'Henry!' She was totally taken aback. 'But Henry – Wetherall doesn't adjoin on Emmerdale at any point—'

Henry rubbed a hand across his pink scalp. 'So much the better, lass. Joe can run Rowan Farm and Jack can run Hathersage's and between them all they can run Emmerdale.'

'But what would it cost, lad? To buy Rowan Farm?'

'More than we've got – or could raise in the ordinary

144

way. But we could find the money.'

'I don't see how . . . '

'We'd have to take out a mortgage on Emmerdale Farm.'

'Never!'

Henry frowned. 'You wanted me to find a way to keep Joe here, Annie. Well, this is it.'

'Mortgage Emmerdale?'

'It's just a way of utilizing a valuable asset, lass. The freehold of Emmerdale is worth a packet, but of course we don't want to sell. We just want to realize some of its value. It would still be ours, and the value is likely to go up rather than down so we'd be borrowing money at an advantage.'

'But what about repayments, Henry?'

'Well, we'd have to farm Rowan in the most profitable way so as to make enough out of it to repay the loan and give Joe a decent wage. We'd have to choose crops that are at a guaranteed high price.'

'But Jack likes to grow only what he considers—'

'Annie, if we're going to kow-tow to Jack's prejudices we might as well give up at the start. If we buy Rowan Farm we'll be about doubling the acreage, and we can't afford to have high-flown notions of what's right and what's wrong. It's a case of making a living for Joe and showing a profit for the mortgage repayments. I would think Jack will go along when he thinks it over. It'll mean a bigger farm, bigger turnover, no problem over fitting Joe into the staff, and even make a bit to finance the "organic" methods on Hathersage. What's wrong wi' that?'

'Nothing . . . '

'What's worrying you, then?'

'It's nothing I can put a finger on, Henry. I just feel it in my bones that Jack won't like it.'

So it proved, though Henry didn't actually have an opportunity to put the plan to Jack. Jack came by at least part of the news by a different method.

He popped into the Woolpack after his evening meal, to find Joe and give him some information. Joe greeted him with a slight smile. 'Come to buy me a consolation drink?' he asked.

'You what?'

'To make it up to me for being thrown out on my ear.'

'Nay, that's not going to happen!' Jack said with complete conviction. 'You're going to take this job that's on offer, aren't you?'

'You reckon I should?'

'Well, why not?' Jack rejoined, raising his black eyebrows in surprise. 'You didn't expect to stick all your life in Beckindale, did you?'

'Didn't I? I kind of thought I would . . .'

'Gerron wi' thee! Beckindale isn't the be-all and end-all of life. There's a lot of England worth looking at – to say nowt of places abroad.'

'You reckon I should go to Rome, eh? Try my hand at film-making in Cinecitta?'

'We-ell . . . I tried that and got fed up of it. But this job Meadowes is offering might take you to some part of England that you'd like, and I daresay you'd be learning summat.'

'Aye, how to survive in a big-scale organization dominated by computers.'

'It sounds a bit daunting.' Jack accepted his bitter from Amos and went on to what had brought him there. 'Speaking of big-scale – you heard the rumour that Stan Wetherall is selling up?'

'It's not a rumour, it's fact. Seth'll tell you.'

Seth, farther along the bar and eavesdropping as much as he could, nodded when Jack glanced at him for confirmation. 'Going to retire in the summer, old Stan,' he said.

'So . . . That accounts for your Mr Meadowes snooping about at the boundaries of Rowan Farm.'

'Was he?' Joe said, interested. 'He never misses a trick! How could he have heard about Stan retiring?'

'You can bet a firm that size has its contacts everywhere – estate agents would give them first refusal of a piece of

146

land like that. Though why the dickens they want it, *I* can't fathom.'

'What d'you mean, you can't fathom? It's obvious. Modern farming methods work better the bigger the spread.'

'Huh! Better? A thing so bad can only get worse,' Jack said.

'Oh, hold on now. Being big isn't necessarily a bad thing. It'd do Emmerdale good to be a bit bigger—'

'Nothing of the kind! Emmerdale is just the right size to give a decent living—'

'Oh, really?' Joe said with apparent innocence. 'I thought there were problems at the moment.'

'That's only temporary! Henry's sorting it for us. After we're on an even keel again, we'll be fine.'

Joe could have said – but did not – that Emmerdale had been on an even keel when he handed it over to his elder brother. Instead he asked: 'Aren't you tempted by the idea of adding a farm like Rowan to Emmerdale's spread? It would give you a far better turnover.'

'I'm not particularly interested in turnover. That's only a book-keeping myth, anyhow.'

'Turnover's a myth? Are you serious?'

'All those terms that you've been brainwashed with, Joe – they're only business conventions. The fact of the matter is that all we want from Emmerdale is enough to live on for us and the Skilbecks.'

'You're not thinking of hiring me, if I turn down Meadowes' offer?'

Jack stared.

'He might want to send me to John o' Groats, you know. I mightn't fancy it.'

'You're not saying you'd want to come back to Emmerdale?' Jack demanded.

'Why not? It's my home, after all.'

'Oh . . . well . . . I mean, it's where you were born, and all that. But you've got Demdyke now as a home—'

'But there's no land to farm at Demdyke. Wouldn't you

147

think of using my talents at Emmerdale?'

Joe wasn't serious. He knew better than anyone that he and Jack could never work together now. Joe had learned too much to want to take orders from Jack, and Jack had backed himself into his own prejudices to such an extent that he couldn't have borne advice from his younger brother.

'I . . . I never thought you'd want to come back to a small place like Emmerdale after the kind of work you've got used to,' Jack stammered.

'Beggars can't be choosers.'

'Joe, are you seriously asking me for a job?'

Joe shook his head. 'After this conversation, I think I'd be a fool – don't you?'

'Well, I mean . . . I don't want to sound as if I . . . '

'As if you didn't want me. No, I never thought that for a minute,' Joe said with sarcasm. 'Don't worry, big brother. I'm not likely to come crying to you if I find Meadowes is being hardhearted.'

'Then what was all this about?' Jack said, irritated. 'I mean, if you knew you didn't want to come back to Emmerdale—'

'I asked you if you wouldn't think of buying Wetherall's farm. It would be a good investment. That was how it all started.'

'Buy Rowan Farm! We'd never raise the capital.'

'Oh yes you would. Emmerdale with Hathersage is good collateral.'

'If you think I'm letting us in for a millstone round our neck—'

'A good mortgage isn't a millstone, Jack. Thousands of farmers have a mortgage on their land.'

'And thousands of farmers chuck chemicals on it to make enough money to pay back the debt! I'm not getting caught in that trap. Emmerdale as it is now is just about the right size. I've no intentions of enlarging it.'

Joe shrugged and put his empty tankard on the bar. 'Suit yourself,' he said. 'But you don't want NY Estates to get

Rowan Farm, and you don't want it for yourself – you're hard to please, lad. *Somebody'll* buy that land. Think on – you might regret it wasn't you.'

He left, leaving Jack to face the thought that NY Estates might very likely be the purchaser, thus making them the owner of about three-quarters of the land in the dale. It was a thought that didn't please him.

Matt Skilbeck was worrying about Stan Wetherall's land too. 'You see, love,' he told his wife, 'it would make sense for Emmerdale to buy it. I don't know how the money would be found, but it would mean Joe could stop in Beckindale instead of being shunted off by this feller Meadowes. So if there's a board meeting to discuss it, I reckon I ought to vote in favour.'

'But what would it entail?' Dolly asked.

'Dunno. Henry's the one who understands high finance. I reckon he could raise the purchase price.'

'What sort of a sum are we talking about? Is it a lot of money?'

'We-ell,' Matt said, 'arable land is going for about a thousand pounds an acre at the moment.'

'Ooh!' Dolly was taken aback. She nuzzled her chin against Baby Sam's downy head. 'Hear that, Sammy? You're going to inherit a share in a fortune one day, by t'sound of it.'

The baby chuckled and waved a fist. 'He's in favour, any road,' Matt laughed.

'I bet Annie is too,' Dolly rejoined. 'She'd be in favour of owt that could keep Joe in the dale.'

'Aye.' Matt frowned and sighed. 'But it won't be easy if he stays.'

'How d'you mean, love?'

'Well, if he goes on seeing Barbara . . .'

Dolly rose to take the baby to his cot. When she came back she was thoughtful. 'This thing between Babs and Joe is serious, Matt,' she said. 'I chat with her quite a bit, and you can tell she's . . . well, things have changed for her since she became close to Joe.'

'But she's married, Dolly!'

'But that can alter.'

'Only if she goes right against her father's wishes. An' if she does that, Dolly, can you imagine what the situation would be like, the vicar disapproving of her divorce and not regarding it as valid if she and Joe got wed?'

Dolly pursed her lips. 'I like Mr Hinton,' she said, 'but he can't live Babs' life for her. If she and Joe get married, I'm all for it.'

'Oh, you!' Matt said, putting an arm about her and giving her a hug. 'You're just a daft romantic, that's what you are.'

Romantic was not quite the view that was being taken by Pat Sugden over the matter. Jack, back from the Woolpack and getting ready for bed, confirmed to her that the rumour about Stan Wetherall selling up was correct. 'But,' he added, 'Joe took my breath away by asking me if he could come back to Emmerdale.'

'He never!' gasped his wife.

'Well . . . no . . . he didn't, really. But he sort of led me on to think he wanted to, and then when he'd seen for certain that I wouldn't like it, he said he wouldn't have wanted to.'

'You mean, he was having you on?'

'I'm not sure,' Jack said, shaking his head and feeling less than pleased with himself.

'Would you offer him a job if this thing with NY proves to be bad for him?' Pat asked, pausing in the act of applying moisturizer. 'I mean, he wouldn't want to take some rotten office job at Lincoln, I imagine.'

'No, he wouldn't. But as for having him here . . . '

'You wouldn't like that?'

'What could he do?' Jack burst out. 'We don't farm on the scale of NY. His ideas wouldn't fit any more.'

'But with this sorting-out that Henry's doing . . . I mean, Joe and Henry have a lot in common, their way of thinking's similar.'

'Are you saying Joe would go over my head to Henry?'

Pat drew back a little, then gave her thoughts. 'You've got to remember that Joe's as much a partner of Emmerdale Farm Limited as you are, love,' she said quietly. 'If it came to a board decision and he and Henry voted for it, and Ma did – and she would, you know!'

'And so would Matt,' Jack said.

'That would mean four to one against you, lad.'

Jack sat silent on the side of the bed, one shoe in his hand and the other still waiting to be taken off.

'What would you do, Jack?' Pat asked.

'I'd have to accept it,' he said. He began to untie the lace of his second shoe. 'Well, happen I'm making a mountain out of a molehill. Happen Joe meant it when he said he wouldn't want to come back to Emmerdale.'

They dropped the subject. But it was in both their minds as they got into bed that rather than have to work as partner with Joe, Jack was likely to throw it all up and leave Emmerdale.

Henry Wilks decided to do nothing further about raising money to buy Wetherall's land until he heard the decision on Joe's future. That was announced to Joe on Friday morning. Joe was called to the office at Home Farm soon after nine o'clock, when he had just finished supervising some livestock-loading at Ridge Farm.

'Come in, Joe. Sit down,' Meadowes said with some affability as Joe came in.

'Thanks.'

'Well now, young man, I gave you a week in which to think over what I said last time we met. I wonder if you've come to any decision?'

'It's difficult to come to a decision when you're being asked to take a leap into the dark, Mr Meadowes.'

'Oh?' The director looked faintly surprised at the acerbity in Joe's voice. 'Surely you understood that I'd be offering you something substantial?'

'I understood only that I had to take everything on trust.'

151

'That's no bad thing, Joe.'

'Trust is a two-way business, Mr Meadowes.'

Aha, thought Arnold Meadowes. This young man is getting a touch of steel about him!

'I understand only too well,' he said, taking a new tack, 'that you haven't had the easiest of times with Alan Turner. Various reports that he sent in to HQ now bear a different interpretation, now that I've been on the spot for myself. The point I want to make here is that you stuck it out uncomplainingly. You could, if you had liked, have made a big issue over the losses at the pig unit—'

'Don't think I didn't consider it!'

'But you decided against. I liked that. It showed loyalty, even to a man who perhaps had not quite deserved it.'

'Mr Meadowes, I didn't come here for a review of the past. The point now is my future, isn't it?'

'Quite, quite. You're understandably anxious. Well, I think I can safely say that your future with NY Estates is very bright, Joe.' He picked up some papers lying before him on the desk. 'You did excellently on that course in Perth, you came up unaided with the idea for the new pig breeding unit, and I gather from looking at the farm where you formerly were manager that you have good experience with sheep.'

'Yes?' Joe said.

'We want to capitalize on that. Livestock raising is one of our prime interests. You'll have read in the company reports that we went into breeding Charollais cattle quite extensively.'

'Yeah, I read that,' Joe put in, his interest quickened so that he forgot his own problems for a moment. 'Those bulls certainly make a difference to the meat production figures—'

'Yes, and their health record is another factor in their favour. I'm glad you show an interest, Joe, because it's in that respect that I want to use your talents.'

'Breeding Charollais?' Joe said, trying to call to mind where the Charollais herd was kept.

'Not to beat about the bush, I'd like you to spend a year on our beef ranch in France, getting to know how things work there. When you've completed that training the situation will be reviewed and it's then highly likely, with this experience behind you, that you'll be offered a senior post with NY Estates.'

He paused. Joe Sugden was looking at him as if he expected him to grow another head.

'It's an exciting prospect, Joe. New work in a new setting, with promotion almost guaranteed at the end of it. What do you say?'

But Joe was at a loss for words.

Chapter Twelve

When Joe told Barbara his news, he could see it was a great blow. 'France! I never even imagined a thing like that.'

'Neither did I, Babs. But though I couldn't take it in at first, I see now that it's a big thing for me.'

They were in the living room at Demdyke. Barbara should have been preparing their evening meal, but Joe's words had put it right out of her head.

'You want to go?'

'Well . . . nay, I can't say I actually *want* to go. But that beef ranch they've got there – I mean, it's got all the latest methods – and pedigree Charollais – and you see, it's a sort of international base – I'd meet experts from all over the world.'

It was easy to see that, for all its drawbacks of strange-ness and foreign-ness, it attracted him.

But Barbara was seeing it from her own point of view. 'I don't even speak French, Joe!'

'Nor do I.' He hesitated. 'I thought you probably would, though.'

'Oh, schoolgirl stuff – the coffee is in the cup – that's about it. And I can ask for a ticket on the Metro.'

'Well, that's more than I can!'

'But there'd be no Metro where you're going, Joe. I take it it's a big farm, if you're calling it a ranch?'

'Oh aye – acres of it.'

'Is there a town?'

'Well, I gather the nearest town is Tours.'

'Nearest? How far is "nearest"?'

'Dunno for sure. About thirty miles, I reckon.'

Barbara had a brief mental picture of herself marooned thirty miles from the nearest town, in a rural community where she couldn't even speak the language.

154

'What on earth would I do with myself?'

'Oh.' That hadn't occurred to him so far. He'd been so busy trying to gather information about the place and what his own job might be that he'd failed to imagine the circumstances for a wife – well, not exactly a wife. But the French were easygoing about that sort of thing, he had heard.

'You could get a job in the office, like you have here.'

'Oh yes? Handling computerese in French? You must be joking, Joe.'

'But . . . I mean . . . there's bound to be correspondence in English, Babs. I mean to say, there's Australians and Canadians from NY's international branches – I met a feller from Queensland at that seminar in Perth, who was going to the French outfit.'

She could see that for the people actually engaged in the farming work, there could be companionship and interests in common. But for wives or living-partners, it wouldn't be so much fun, unless the woman was a Francophile to start with.

And Barbara was not. The only interest she had in common with the French was food and wine. When she'd gone on holidays abroad with Brian, they'd always headed for Greece – France had never attracted them except for occasional weekends in Paris.

Paris she liked – because it was one of the most beautiful cities in the world. She was a city girl, which was why she'd never been able to feel happy in Beckindale until she began to form a relationship with Joe. She had to admit to herself that had Joe not been around, by now she'd probably have left for Manchester or London to find a job worthy of her abilities.

But as for burying herself again in the heart of the countryside – and the French countryside at that! – it just sounded too remote, too awful. It was too big a step to take. She thought she loved Joe – was almost sure she did – but it was too early to commit herself to him in such a total way. Thrown together in a rural setting in a foreign

155

country! What could be a worse start to any permanent relationship? she asked herself.

'It's not for me, Joe,' she said. 'I couldn't take it.'

'If I can find out a bit more about it – I mean, there might be a decent-sized village.'

She shook her head. 'No. I don't even think I'd be in Beckindale except for circumstances turning out the way they have. I'm certainly not interested in the equivalent of Beckindale in the midst of the French countryside.'

'You really wouldn't go?'

'No.'

There was a pause. 'Okay,' said Joe. 'Then I won't go.'

She was appalled at what she had done. 'Don't be silly, Joe!' she cried. 'This is a wonderful chance for you! You can't throw it away just because I—'

'I'm not being silly.' He took her hand. 'I want you more than any job, Babs. If it's a choice between you and France, then France gets the elbow.'

'No! No, don't put me in this position! It's not fair!'

'How d'you mean?' he countered, genuinely puzzled. 'I'm not doing owt to you, love. I'm just telling you that—'

'You're telling me that it depends on me, what happens to your career.'

'Well, of course! If we're to have a future—'

'Oh, please! Don't! It's *your* future we're talking about.'

'It's our future.'

'But it's not *fair*, Joe—'

'What's fair got to do with it?' he broke in. 'I love you, Barbara. You're the chief thing.'

'But you can't sacrifice your career for me.'

'Why not? You're more important than my career.'

'I'm not, Joe! Listen—'

'*I'm* the one who decides what's important to me!'

'But you've no right to load me with the responsibility! It's like putting a gun to my head! "Come with me or I'll finish my life".'

'*You're* my life, Barbara.'

Suddenly she took refuge in anger. 'For God's sake stop

156

trying to be poetic about it!' she cried. 'It's not poetic nor sensible to make decisions affecting your whole life on emotions – believe me, I know!'

'What are you saying now?' he asked in alarm. 'Are you talking about the decision to leave Brian? You think it was a mistake?'

'I'm not talking about that. I'm talking about us. We've only known each other a few months. If you'd really lived with me, seen me with my hair in a tangle, slopping about in the morning with no make-up—'

'Oh, come on, Babs!'

'I mean it! We've been on best behaviour with each other, don't pretend we haven't!'

'But I've seen you first thing in the morning. And I like you without make-up.'

'Oh, that wears off, Joe!' There was bitterness in her voice. 'That first complete approval gets replaced by a little feeling of criticism. You know it, so do I – you soon see the faults in your partner and get irritated.'

He studied her. 'You think I'd get irritated first? Or you?' There was a glint of amusement in his eyes as he said it. Then, to show how little he thought of her argument, he put his arms about her and drew her very close, kissing her hard.

It was a good way of getting the better of her. As she felt the familiar warmth of his body she melted towards him. But then that common sense that had always been an important part of her character made her struggle free.

'Don't, Joe – this isn't how to settle things.'

'Seems a good way to me.'

'It's not sensible—'

'Come on, now, love – this is above profit-and-loss accounts and sensible attitudes. You love me. I love you. That won't wear off.' He stroked her cheek with his rough palm. 'Will it?'

She started back, and headed for the door. 'I'm not going to stop here talking about it if you're going to use physical need as an argument—'

'Babs!'

But she was gone. He realized she was heading out of the gate when he heard it creak as she opened it.

She'd be back, though. And by then she'd have had time to think things over.

Either way, he was sure she'd see they needed each other. He didn't care how the thing was settled – either they went to France together or he found a job here. But one thing he was sure of: his future lay with Barbara.

His future was that moment receiving earnest consideration at Emmerdale. The other partners of Emmerdale Farm Limited were holding a meeting to discuss the astounding news that Joe had phoned to his mother earlier that evening.

'Jack, you'd never want Joe to go and live in France,' Annie was urging her elder son.

'Good heavens, it's not for ever, Ma! As I understand it, it's a year's training.'

'A year,' she echoed in dismay.

'It's not so long.'

'It is at my age, son,' she cut him off. 'And your grandad – every year's precious to him, and a year wi'out Joe would be a terrible loss.'

'Look, I want to go along with any scheme to help have Joe here,' Jack said, trying to keep the irritation out of his voice. He felt he was being cast in the role of villain just because he didn't approve of Henry's notions. 'I just hate the idea of us being saddled with the kind of debt Henry's got in mind.'

'It's not a *debt*,' Henry rejoined, irritated too. Why couldn't the man see things in a sensible businesslike way? 'We have the assets to back it.'

'I don't understand that kind of talk and I don't want to! To me, owing money is a debt, even if it's backed by owning the Bank of England!'

Matt could see the other two men were growing annoyed

with each other. He broke in with: 'There's sense in what Henry's saying, Jack. A man's not really in debt if he owns more'n he owes. I mean, we could repay the loan any time.'

'Only by selling Emmerdale—'

'Nay, Jack, we wouldn't have to sell everything up to repay—'

'What you're saying is we could sell Hathersage if we had to. I know none of you've ever really approved.'

'We wouldn't have to sell owt,' Henry said flatly. 'We'd make a good profit with Rowan Farm and repay the mortgage that way.'

'But only if it's farmed to the utmost.'

'Well, what's wrong with that? It's how most farmers go on, lad. Not many men can afford to let an asset lie idle.'

'Hathersage isn't idle! It's under pasture now.'

'We're not talking about Hathersage. Nothing we're saying now is intended as a criticism of Hathersage. What we're saying is that Rowan Farm would make a profitable addition to Emmerdale and we could make money by farming it in the modern way.'

'With Joe bringing in all his chemicals and machinery?'

'Joe's got more sense than do owt over-zealous with Rowan Farm. And to have a bigger holding gives us advantages in dealing.'

'I bet there's many a bankrupt has said that kind of thing, Henry!'

'Business is founded on "that kind of thing", lad. And that's what we're in – business.'

'And because you enjoy business, you want to make us big and important, is that it?'

Henry gritted his teeth. 'I could take that as an insult, Jack, but I won't. I give you credit for more sense than to believe I'm just trying to make myself look big.'

Jack looked a little shamed, but wouldn't withdraw it. 'It's a disease with businessmen, though, isn't it?' he muttered. 'To always want to be bigger.'

'You're interested in the natural way of things,' Matt put in, once again acting peacemaker. 'In nature, anything that

159

isn't growing is likely to be dying – now isn't that a fact? Hardly anything stays stationary – it grows or it goes under.'

'Aye, and likely that's what'll happen to us if we outreach ourselves – we'll go under!'

'You mean you're afraid to take on extra commitments – is that it, Jack?' his mother asked.

'Afraid? I'm not afraid. I just disapprove, that's all.'

'It wouldn't be that you don't want to see yourself in a real partnership with Joe? I mean, up to now, Joe's let you go along your own sweet way with Emmerdale and Hathersage. Do you feel you couldn't hold your end up if he was in active partnership?'

Jack stared at his mother. It was very close to open criticism of his attitude. All at once he saw it from her viewpoint – she was about to lose her younger son for a year, simply because Jack wouldn't relent in his opposition.

He pulled himself together. 'I'm sorry,' he began again to Henry. 'I didn't mean to be personal in what I said. You know I don't like the concept of farming as a business. To me, it's a way of life, or should be. If you make it into a business you ruin it – you make it a factory in the fields.'

Wilks sighed. 'Farming is what it is, Jack. It's a way of making a living.'

'It's a way of living,' Jack corrected, 'a way of life. It's a home. You don't run a home for profit and efficiency – you run it for the happiness of the family.'

'All right, Jack,' Matt said. 'The happiness of the family gets less, doesn't it, if the family gets broken up? Or if not enough money's coming in for them to have decent food and to keep the children clothed? We need to keep Joe with us in Beckindale – that's what this is about. And the only way to do it is to buy from Stan Wetherall and make a space for Joe. And the only way we can do it is by following Henry's way, as far as I can see.'

'The only way we can raise the money is to mortgage the freehold of Emmerdale. We should have done it long ago,' Henry said stoutly. 'It's an under-used asset.'

160

Jack cast a bitter glance at his mother. 'We live in an asset, you see,' he declared. 'It's not a home!'

'Oh, for Pete's sake, Jack!' Henry broke out, half getting up from his chair.

'Nay, nay, stay where you are, Henry,' Annie said, laying a hand on his sleeve. 'We've got to sort this. Joe's future's at stake here.'

'I don't take it back,' Jack said. 'I can't see Emmerdale as an "asset". To me it's a home. It's an attitude of mind that keeps us from agreeing, Henry.'

'Of course it is.' Henry had subsided into his chair again and, in deference to Annie, was making a big attempt to come to terms with Jack. 'And my attitude is different from yours – but you mustn't think I'm ashamed of it, because I'm not. My view of the world is what makes it tick. If we all just sat in our houses and made just enough to get by, there'd be no society, no civilization. Farming the land may be the basis of life but it's not the whole of it.'

'It's the whole of life here,' Jack insisted. 'It's what makes Emmerdale important—'

'Excuse me, it's not the only thing that makes Emmerdale important,' Henry said. 'You want to learn to hold opinions without putting a halo round 'em, lad! I like to use my mind, and my mind is as important to me as ploughing a field is to you – but I can't enjoy my way of life if I'm to fall in with all your wishes. I'm chairman of Emmerdale Farm Limited – you gave me that role yourself because you preferred not to handle the business side—'

'But I only meant the day-to-day affairs! I never meant us to get involved in big transactions.'

'Jack,' his mother said, 'what kind of transaction do you think it was when we bought Hathersage?'

Jack stared at her. For a moment he went pale, then he coloured up. 'You're saying I'm selfish.'

'I'm saying that it seemed to be all right to buy extra land when you wanted to but not now that we need it for Joe.'

Jack looked at Matt. 'You don't think Hathersage was a mistake, do you, Matt?'

Matt hesitated. He liked to tell the truth at all times. He couldn't say he thought Hathersage had been a total blessing but by the time he'd framed what he felt was tactful, Jack had nodded to himself.

'I see. So we have to buy Rowan Farm to compensate for my mistakes, is that it?'

'That's not it, Jack, and you know it,' Annie said. 'We need to buy Rowan Farm to give summat for Joe to turn to – and don't forget, he's an equal partner in Emmerdale Farm, and has as much right to a living as any of us.'

'Of course I accept that.'

'All right, if you accept he has a right to a living, tell us how to get it for him – if you've a better plan than Henry's, let's hear it.'

'We can make a place for Joe,' Jack insisted. 'All we have to do is tighten our belts.'

Henry frowned. Any belt-tightening would not, of course, affect him. But for Annie it could be hard going, and as for Matt and Dolly and their baby . . . He looked at Matt.

Matt said: 'I don't want to seem out for myself. But I don't want to see my standard o' living go down, Jack. It's not as if we exactly live on the fat o' the land even now.'

'And what if Joe were to marry?' Henry put in.

'And another thing,' Annie broke in with haste. She didn't want to get side-tracked on to that possibility – she knew Jack would say that Barbara Peters was as yet a married woman, that any marriage with Joe was at least a year ahead. 'This is summat that ought to interest you, lad, and it's nowt to do with Joe's situation. If we don't buy Wetherall's land, who will?'

Her son stared at her, completely at a loss. 'Hey-up!' said Matt. 'I see what you mean, Ma!'

'What?' asked Jack. 'I don't understand—'

'NY Estates will buy Wetherall's if we don't. You know they want to . . . what-you-ma-callit . . . consolidate their position in the Dales.'

Jack threw himself back in his chair with a gesture of

disgust. 'Why have we been wasting our time here?' he exclaimed. 'I think the money Henry's been suggesting is astronomical, but NY could outbid us for Rowan Farm any time they liked.'

'Nay.' Henry was shaking his head. 'Stan and I have an agreement. If Emmerdale want his land, the price he and I discussed is a firm arrangement. Stan isn't going to listen to anything from anyone else until he gets a yea or nay from us.'

'That's right good of him,' Matt said. 'He's always been a straight lad, has Stan.'

'But of course, if we decide against, it only makes sense for him to sell to the highest bidder. You'll be a little island in a sea of NY property, Jack. How'll you like that?'

Jack jutted his chin. 'I'm not afraid of NY.'

'Never said you were. But you'll have to be civil to 'em if you want to have any influence on 'em. If they decide to level every dyke and grub out every hedgerow all around your land, you can't stop 'em—'

'Henry, don't!' Matt begged. 'The idea makes me feel the cold wind already. Can you imagine the effect it'd have on our livestock, Jack – no shelter from that north-easter?'

'And there's the business of approach roads. Alan Turner was telling me NY would like to build a surfaced road to their pig unit – if they get Stan's property I expect they'll get permission to build a road.'

The thought of the disturbance to Emmerdale's life was dreadful. Jack sighed. 'All right,' he said. 'You've painted a picture that makes me see we should own Wetherall's land, not NY.'

'I'm putting it to the vote,' said Henry at once. 'The motion is that we mortgage Emmerdale and buy Stan Wetherall's property. All in favour?'

There was a pause.

'I'd like this to be unanimous,' Henry said, looking straight at Jack. 'It's a big step – I don't want it said later that there were divisions among us. Now – all in favour?'

'Aye,' said Annie.

'Aye,' said Matt.

Jack didn't speak. But he raised his hand and nodded his head.

'The minutes will show that all were agreed,' said Henry. 'Does anyone dispute that, before I go any further?'

'No, Henry,' Jack grunted. 'Don't go on about it – you've won. It's what you wanted and you've got it.'

Henry was about to say that it would never have entered his head to bid for Wetherall's, except that Annie had asked him to help keep Joe at Emmerdale. But Annie forestalled him.

'Jack, don't be so ungracious,' she said in a very cool tone. 'It's what all the rest of us wanted – me most of all. If thou's a bone to pick, pick it wi' me!'

Jack got up. 'I won't wrangle with you about it, Ma,' he said. 'I've agreed because I can see there's no other choice. But it won't be the Emmerdale I came home to any more.'

He went out, hands in pockets, shoulders hunched, to find Pat and give her the news. To her it was information whose importance she could only judge by her husband's expression of gloom.

'Never mind, love,' she said. 'It means Joe can stay living at Demdyke and manage Rowan Farm from there. Better than having him breathing down your neck at Emmerdale, eh?'

When it was put that way, it sounded smallminded. Jack felt a twinge of remorse. But the plain fact was, he didn't want Joe here at Emmerdale. He might talk about making a place for him by tightening their belts, but it wasn't in his nature to accept advice or opinions from a man he still thought of as his kid brother.

Yet to have let himself be elbowed into what he always referred to sneeringly as 'aggro-business'. He could foresee all kinds of problems. There would have to be a better style of book-keeping, more auditing, more control over any plans he might have for Hathersage . . .

It almost made him feel ready to chuck it all up and move on again.

But that wasn't so easy now. He had a wife and family to think of now.

Henry sought out Joe to give him the news. 'We decided in favour of buying, lad.'

'You mean Jack actually agreed?'

'After some discussion – aye.'

Joe laughed. 'I bet it was a heated discussion.'

'Aye, generated more heat than light. But never you mind, lad. We've put matters in hand to give you a career here in Beckindale.'

Joe considered it. 'I wonder if Barbara would like that better?'

'Better than what?'

'Going to France. She seems dead against that.'

Henry looked at him with interest. 'You don't seem so "anti" as you were at first, Joe?'

'Well . . . I've found out a bit about the place. They've got a thousand head of cattle there . . . It's like nowt I've ever seen. And pedigree breeding to a standard you don't get in this country – I mean, there's a team of scientists keeping the records.'

'Sounds a big thing.'

'Oh aye, it's big – and the thing is, Henry, it leads on to even bigger things, for me I mean. They're talking about opening a place here in England, probably in Shropshire, to do the same thing on a smaller scale. You know, Henry, they might even give that to me, if I were to do well in France.'

Henry pushed aside the lager Joe had poured for him from a can from his fridge. 'Let's get this straight, Joe. Are you saying you'd rather go and try this new thing in France, rather than stay and farm Rowan?'

A long silence ensued, in which Joe poured his own lager. He set it down without attempting to sample it. 'I'll be honest, Henry. If I stay here and farm Rowan, I'm only doing what I've always done so far. I'm not knocking it, it's good work and I'm good at it. But . . . '

'Go on.'

'If I go to France, the sky's the limit. It's all new, it's a challenge, I might end up at the front of the new farming industry.'

'You'd like that?'

'It's not a thing to turn your back on without thinking.'

'I'd like to know your decision, as soon as possible, Joe. I can't commit myself to a handshake with Stan Wetherall and then find you'd rather go and breed Charollais.'

Joe shook his head in doubt. 'It doesn't depend on me. It depends on Babs.'

'And what do you think she'll want to do?'

'Well, she certainly doesn't want to go to France – she made that clear enough. And I sort of wonder . . . '

'What?'

'She kept saying she was a city girl. You know, I don't think she really likes country life.'

'What you're saying is that living at Demdyke while you farm Rowan is no marvellous alternative for her.'

Joe didn't answer. He sipped his lager.

Henry said: 'Sorry, son. I can't provide any other solution. I've come up with this thing with Stan Wetherall because it's summat I can do – it's a matter of making a good investment, seeing assets properly used. But I can't provide a career for you in a city where you can follow your ambitions and Barbara can be happy.'

Joe nodded. 'You've been a marvel so far, Henry. I'm not expecting you to solve this.' He looked upset. 'I don't quite see how it's to be solved, to tell the truth.'

'Tell Barbara about Rowan Farm. Happen that'll please her more than you think.'

'I can't tell her. I don't know where she is. I thought she'd gone home to the vicarage but I rang there and Mr Hinton said she got into her car and drove off.' He looked at the clock. 'It's getting late. I thought she'd have been back by now.'

166

Henry could tell that he'd stumbled into the middle of a big emotional mix-up. While he finished his drink, he chatted about possibilities with Wetherall's land, but then took his leave as soon as he could. Amos had had to manage on his own this evening, would by now have locked up, and would be lying in bed listening for him to come home so that he could put his head round the door and complain about the noise he made.

At about eleven o'clock the phone rang at Demdyke. 'It's me,' Barbara's voice said. 'I didn't want you to worry. I've taken a room for the night at the Feathers.'

'You're in Connelton?' Joe exclaimed. 'What the heck are you doing there?'

'I'm trying to think, Joe.'

'Good lord, couldn't you think here?'

'No, I couldn't! Nor at home with Daddy either! Nobody ever leaves me alone to make up my own mind!'

There was something almost childlike in the tone. Joe, who had been quite angry at first, relented. 'All right, love, I won't hassle you. Have a good night's sleep and happen in the morning your mind'll be clear about what you want to do. But there's summat I want to tell you – it changes things for us.'

'Changes? How do you mean?'

'Henry and the others have decided to buy Stan Wetherall's property.'

'They'll never get it,' she cut in. 'Mr Meadowes was showing an interest in that.'

'Henry's got Stan's promise of first refusal. They'll get it. So you see, love, we don't have to go to France. We can stop here and farm Rowan Farm.'

He waited anxiously for her reply. When it came, it put him in an awkward spot.

'Is that what you want?' she asked. 'To farm another farm in the Dales? I thought you were attracted to the prospects NY were holding out.'

'Yes, but you know I only want to do what you want to do.'

167

'I *told* you, Joe! Don't say things like that! Don't put it all on to me!'

'Now, now – don't be angry – I'm sorry, Babs.'

'I think we'd better ring off. It's a waste of time, quarrelling by telephone.'

'I don't want to quarrel. I want to agree. Just tell me what you want, love.'

He could hear her sigh of exasperation. 'Goodnight, Joe,' she said, and put the phone down.

She didn't come into the office next day. Alan Turner was furious. 'If she thinks she can just walk in and out like this—'

'Alan, her job's been cut down to nothing. You'd best be careful what you say to her or she won't bother to come in at all.'

'Oh, really? Has she been telling you she's upset about Meadowes' decision, Joe?'

'She's hardly mentioned it.'

'Oh, I see. You just know, by instinct.'

'Don't get snooty with me, Alan. I know what Barbara's feeling at the moment – and let me tell you, this tuppenny-ha'penny job with NY in Beckindale figures nowhere.'

'And what does, pray tell?'

What did? There was no way of knowing. When he rang the hotel to speak to her, he was told she'd gone out for a walk after breakfast.

Jack Sugden had business in Connelton that day – or at least he persuaded himself he had, so as to get away from the atmosphere at Emmerdale. Matt wanted to talk about the new outlook that would come when they owned Rowan Farm, Pat wondered if they could use the farmhouse at Rowan as a home, and even his grandfather was making drawings to show young Jackie how he could walk from Emmerdale to Rowan without entering NY land.

Jack wanted to buy a birthday present for Pat. He wandered round the rather smart shops of Connelton, without an idea in his head. At length he went into the coffee shop attached to the pottery, and there he found Barbara Peters.

'Hello,' he said with more warmth than he actually felt. He had liked her well enough when she first came to Beckindale but now she was simply part of his problem – the girl Joe would probably marry, the girl for whose sake Joe had to have a decent home to offer in Beckindale.

'Oh, hello, Jack. I didn't expect to see you here.'

He gave the excuse about birthday presents and was rewarded with two or three good ideas. The waitress came, he ordered coffee and scones.

'What are you doing here?' he asked when the girl had gone.

'Escaping.'

'From what?'

'Pressure.'

He gave a little laugh. 'I know what you mean! Well, I won't pressure you about anything, you can be sure of that. I've suffered.'

'Oh?' She was quick to catch on. 'You mean, about buying Rowan Farm?'

'You know about that?'

'Joe told me on the phone.'

'It's a bad decision, though it was a case of "lesser of two evils",' Jack said, following his own train of thought. 'Now I'll have that damned mortgage hanging round my neck for the next twenty years! It means that we'll all have to be terribly, terribly careful – never any chance to try something just for the hell of it!'

She smiled at him. 'I don't think farming these days is done much "for the hell of it", Jack.'

'That's what's wrong with it! It's turning into a monster – destroying the country again just as the first Industrial Revolution did. The first time, all the people were driven off into the towns. This time, all the vitality is being drained away into ledgers and computers.'

'You really feel as badly as that about it?'

169

'When I let myself think about it, I do! I'll tell you one thing,' he said, thumping the table softly with his fist, 'I'll never forgive Joe for this! If he'd take that job NY's offering, there'd be no need to turn our lives upside down – but no, he's got to have something worthwhile to turn to and so we're tied up in a financial deal that I absolutely hate!'

The waitress came with his order. He found to his surprise that he was hungry, having eaten very little breakfast so as to get away from the chat at the breakfast table. He didn't talk much while he satisfied his hunger and didn't notice that Barbara seemed to have very little to say either. As he was pouring his second cup of coffee she rose to go.

'Oh, won't you have another, just to keep me company?'

'No thanks, I'd better get home. Daddy'll be worried sick about me by now.'

Her father was out on parish business when she got to the vicarage. She packed quickly, then drove to Demdyke to get those items that had inevitably found a home there.

Then she went to find Joe. He was at Ridge Farm, arguing with the vet about a suspected injury to one of the pedigree cows.

He turned away at once to join her. 'Babs! I'm right glad to see you—'

'I've come to tell you what I've decided, Joe,' she said. 'It's only fair to tell you at once.'

'What?' he said, alarmed by her tone.

'I've decided to go back to Brian.'

'Brian? Babs, you can't!'

'I haven't come to have an argument. I just wanted to let you know. Goodbye, Joe.'

'But – wait – Barbara.'

He hurried after her. She got into her car. '*Barbara!*'

'It's no use, Joe,' she said through the open window, safe inside the steely shelter of the car. 'It never was any use. I see now I thought I was in love with you because I needed to feel *something* – but it was just love on the rebound.'

'But you don't love Brian—'

'Don't I?' she asked with a faint smile. 'Then why am I going back to him?' She rolled up the window and drove off without so much as a wave of farewell, leaving Joe standing by the side of the road, white and stricken.

She reached the vicarage again as her father was coming in, his arms full of newly covered hymnbooks.

'Barbara! My dear! I'm so glad you've come back—'

'I've just come to say goodbye, Daddy. I'm leaving Beckindale.'

'My dear child!'

'My luggage is in the car. I'm leaving straight away.'

'But, but – what about Joe?'

'I've spoken to Joe.'

'What did you say to him?' the vicar demanded, bewildered.

'I told him I'm going back to Brian.'

Her father's face lit up. 'Oh, my dear girl, that's such good news!' He hastily pushed the hymnbooks on to the edge of the hall table. He turned to her, putting out his hands to take hers. She drew back, but he swept on: 'I'm sure you and Brian can make a go of it. He wants to, I know – and if you pull together—'

'Daddy, it was a lie.'

'What?'

'What I told Joe – it was a lie. I'm not going back to Brian. I've decided to try my luck in London.'

Donald Hinton was totally at a loss. 'But why? I don't understand!'

'I'm a hindrance to Joe's career. I didn't want to go with him to France, so at Emmerdale they cooked up some scheme to keep him here in Beckindale. But his brother hates the idea, it puts them in debt for the next twenty years—'

'Oh, I'm sure Henry Wilks would take care—'

'It's not the money – it was the resentment in Jack's voice when he said he'd never forgive Joe. I couldn't be part of that. Besides, the time would come when Joe would regret

171

giving up that wonderful chance with NY Estates. And then – perhaps I'm selfish, but I'm scared of being hustled into a relationship so soon. I . . . I just don't think I could handle it.'

He put his arms about her and held her close, stroking her hair with the palm of his hand. It was as if she was a child again, coming to him for comfort when she had bruised her knee. Yet, though he was deeply sorry for her, he was happy too. She had drawn back from a great sin. Who could tell – perhaps she and her husband would mend their marriage. The Almighty had certainly given her a second chance.

Joe Sugden came knocking at the door only half an hour after she had gone. It had taken him just that long to get rid of the vet, find his Land Rover, and drive down to the village. 'I'm sorry, Joe,' Hinton said. 'She's gone.'

'Back to her husband?'

'She told you so, I think?'

Joe nodded. Hinton had an impulse to tell him the truth, for the boy looked really ill. Yet prudence held him back. He let the unspoken lie hold sway.

'I see,' Joe said. 'Well . . . when she rings or anything, tell her . . . tell her I wish her all the luck in the world.'

'I'll do that, Joe.'

Joe walked to the Woolpack. He hardly saw the pavement on which he trod, though his gaze seemed to be fixed on it. Henry was busy at the bar but, when Joe beckoned, lifted the flap and slipped out to join him.

'Mr Wilks!' complained Amos. 'There's customers—'

'Dry up, Amos. Can't you see it's summat important?'

Joe had gone outside into the warm sunshine of late May. Henry fell into step with him as he moved off. 'Have you spoken to Stan Wetherall yet, Henry?'

'Nay. I were waiting for you to say the word.'

'I've come to say it – and it's no. Don't buy Rowan Farm. I've decided to go to France.'

'You what?' Henry gasped. 'Barbara changed her mind?'

'Aye, you could say so. She's gone back to sort out her marriage.'

Henry was silenced. At length he said, 'I'm sorry, lad. I can see it's a blow.'

'Aye. Well . . . it simplifies things from the family point of view. Ma was always worried about how it looked, me and Barbara . . . And Mr Hinton was put in a bad light. And now you don't have to put a mortgage on Emmerdale.' He shrugged. 'Jack'll be pleased.'

'Aye, he will. The more so as I hear Stan Wetherall told Meadowes point blank he wouldn't let him have his land even if Emmerdale didn't want it. Stan wants a Yorkshire farmer to get it.'

Joe wasn't even listening. 'She just didn't like the idea of being a farmer's wife,' he said, as if to himself. 'It's not her fault, and it's not mine – it's just the way things turned out . . .'

They parted at the end of the village street. Joe walked off towards the fells. He felt the need of hard physical exercise, a reaction towards the chill that seemed to hold him since Barbara had driven away.

When he reached the ridge he stood looking down at the village. He had spent his whole life here. He turned his head a little. There, down the dale, in a little fold of the land, was the farmhouse where he'd been born. Probably at this very moment his mother was serving the midday meal, as she'd done a thousand times and more.

Soon that would be behind him. Although he had still to tell his decision to Arnold Meadowes, already he was saying goodbye to Emmerdale.

A new life awaited him, miles away in a foreign land. A year would pass before he would see this view again.

A year in which many changes might happen.